What people are saying about

Too Fat to go to the Moon

This is for another work, "Nixon In Space", but I think Mr. Lethem would agree, "Too Fat to go to the Moon" is just as good as "Nixon In Space", but with the added selling point of featuring public masturbation.

In the annals of baseball, statistics-freaks love talking about the players who came up from the minors and got a single hit, or two, then retired with a batting average of a thousand. (I think I read once of a guy who went 3-for-3 on his sole day in the bigs, the Ty Cobb of one-day-wonders.) Or the pitcher who struck out the only batter he ever faced. Well, I was once party to the writing equivalent—mystery-man Rob McCleary, who offered up one perfect fluttering knuckleball of a short story, "Nixon in Space," then seemingly evaporated. You can barely even Google up evidence the thing existed, apart from a few LiveJournal pages. The reason I know about it is I was once upon a time a regular contributor to CRANK! Magazine, the now-itself-forgotten venue where McCleary offered up his gem, which humbled those of us prematurely jaded veterans who thought we had better stuff than the rookies. The story is exuberant and rageful, political and eccentric, relevant and timeless. If you wrote "Nixon In Space" or its equivalent fifty times you'd be George Saunders or Donald Barthelme. Do it just once and you're Rob McCleary, I guess.

Jonathan Lethem, author of *Fortress of Solitude*

Too Fat to go to the Moon

Gay Sasquatch Saved My Life

Too Fat to go to the Moon

Gay Sasquatch Saved My Life

Rob McCleary

Winchester, UK
Washington, USA

First published by Zero Books, 2019
Zero Books is an imprint of John Hunt Publishing Ltd., No. 3 East St., Alresford,
Hampshire SO24 9EE, UK
office1@jhpbooks.net
www.johnhuntpublishing.com
www.zero-books.net

For distributor details and how to order please visit the 'Ordering' section on our website.

Text copyright: Rob McCleary 2018

ISBN: 978 1 78535 231 7
978 1 78535 232 4 (ebook)
Library of Congress Control Number: 2018931365

A CIP catalogue record for this book is available from the British Library.

Design: Stuart Davies

Printed and bound by CPI Group (UK) Ltd, Croydon, CR0 4YY, UK

We operate a distinctive and ethical publishing philosophy in
all areas of our business, from our global network of authors to
production and worldwide distribution.

Also by Rob McCleary
Nixon in Space

Chapter 1

This is a story about America, and jerking off, not necessarily in that order. It is the story of the Van Kruup family, of whom (full disclosure) I am a member. We were a very important family in America, back when there was still an America to be an important family in. Kennedy important. Rockefeller important. America (if you missed the memo) is no more. The jerking off, in proud, patriotic, flag-saluting towns and cities across what used to be America, I must assume, continues apace (those who cannot remember the past).

$ $ $

This is a story about America, or what's left of it (the parts we didn't sell to the Chinese) and jerking off. It is a memoir. By a President (sort of): I was President of the parts of America we didn't sell to the Chinese to pay to put the Statue of Liberty and the Empire State Building into space. I was once President of the Remaining States of America. I was once the King of New York (hold that thought). I was once the sole heir to the Van Kruup family fortune. Which was founded on jerking off (full circle).

$ $ $

The Van Kruup family was an important family in America back when there was still an America to be an important family in. Unlike the Kennedys or the Rockefellers we were not important by virtue of anything we accomplished or contributed. We were important simply by virtue of our fortune: we had tons and tons and tons of money. And in America, once upon a time, that was virtue enough.

The extended Van Kruup family all lived off The Van Kruup Family Trust (all caps) which was Frankensteined out of the

Van Kruup family fortune. The Van Kruup family fortune was founded on coal, oil, steel, railroads, jerking off, and garbage, not necessarily in that order. Garbage: putting it into space. In rockets. Jerking off: by a midget (or, if you prefer: "little person") dressed in period costume - Napoleon, Kaiser Wilhelm II, Julius Caesar, Henry VIII. That's how our fortune got started: jerking off. Then Father invested the entire contents of The Van Kruup Family Trust in the Funk Market. And the Funk Market crashed. So we were broke. So I had to get a job: jerking off. For paying audiences. For the Kennedys and the Rockefellers. Dressed in period costume: Napoleon, Kaiser Wilhelm II, Julius Caesar, Henry VIII(those who cannot remember the past).

$$\$ \ \$ \ \$$$

This is a story about America and the Van Kruups. America is no more. The Van Kruups are no more. The Rockefellers live and work in the orbiting Empire State Building. Last I heard, the Kennedys had taken to the ocean in JFK's sailing yacht "Manitou" to become a savage, sea-raiding people, pillaging the New England coast and forcing their conquered, vassal subjects to play touch football until they are dead in a sick form of tribute. Most of America got sold to the Chinese. Then the Van Kruups lost every penny in the Great Funk Crash (all caps).

America was destroyed by Trees (capital "T"). Before Trees destroyed America, trying to guess what would destroy America was a national obsession. We were a paranoid, twitchy bunch. The details of our paranoid obsessions changed with the times. We thought thermonuclear war would destroy America. We thought terrorist attacks would destroy America. We thought Ebola would destroy America. We did not think Trees would destroy America. Trees destroyed America. Trees everywhere. A plague of Trees. Sprouting up through our interstates. Short circuiting and stripping our high tension power lines with their flailing, upreaching branches. Burrowing down into the earth with their roots and strangling our sewers and water mains. And it all happened in a single night. The night I was crowned King of New York (hold that thought). Trees destroyed our shopping malls, our highways, our airports runways. All transportation infrastructure: gone, useless, destroyed. Every city or village not located on a navigable body of water is now defunct. Buffalo, on the Erie canal, is booming. Indianapolis, trapped on the arid prairie, is kaput. Indianapolis is now "The Lost City of Indianapolis". Like "The Lost City of Atlantis", which sunk in the ocean and was covered in water. Except The Lost City of Indianapolis was deluged by Trees. Your best bets to get around in America today: canoe, Presidential sailing yacht "Manitou", or dog travois. In conclusion: Trees destroyed America.

$ $ $

Trees destroyed America and the Great Funk Crash destroyed The Van Kruup Family Trust and with it the Van Kruup family. We could no more live without the protective bubble of our fortune than we could walk on the surface of the moon without a space suit. We had no practical skills. We had *one* practical skill: professional rich asshole. But drop the "rich" out of that equation and all you're left with is "professional asshole" (I did the math). That's not entirely true. I had one marketable skill, but I did not discover it until after Funky Friday (the day the Funk Market cratered). I had one practical skill which would save me after the Van Kruup family fortune was demolished and Trees destroyed America and "catamite" became a viable occupation: masturbating, in period costume, dressed as Napoleon, Kaiser Wilhelm II, Julius Caesar, and Henry VIII.

First there was the Great Funk Crash, the Trees came after. In fairness to the Trees, America was kaput a long time before they became the period at the end of the violent, chaotic, rambling run-on sentence that was American history. By the time the Trees showed up, we were broke and had sold Texas, New Mexico, Nevada, Missouri, Kansas, Oklahoma, Michigan and Wisconsin to the Chinese to pay to put the Empire State Building and the Statue of Liberty in space (and here I purse my lips and raise a single finger in the air, the international gesture for "I'll get there eventually"). When the Trees made their move, unless you had a canoe, a dog travois, a Presidential sailing yacht once owned by JFK and restored with a painstaking eye to detail like the Kennedys, or were prepared to walk across half a continent barefoot like Johnny Fucking Appleseed, you were pretty much stuck wherever you were the moment the Trees took over. I got stuck in Albany. In New York State. Where I had just been crowned King of New York. With my twin Irish wolf hounds, Romulus and Remus. And the Duke of Indianapolis. Who, I guess, is now technically The Duke of the Lost City of Indianapolis.

$$\$ \ \$ \ \$$$

It would be difficult to over dramatize America's death spiral. Even before Trees took over I managed to get elected Vice President of the Remaining States of America. Then I was appointed President of the Remaining States of America. I wasn't qualified to be President. I wasn't qualified to be Vice President, and the Vice President doesn't have to be qualified to do *anything*. Then I was crowned King of New York. I didn't even want to be President. I didn't want to be Vice President. I was eager to give the "King of New York" thing a try, but Trees had other plans. The Trees made their move the night of my coronation. Where did the Trees come from? I do not know. After I took the oath of office for President I was shown many things only the President is ever shown. I was taken to Roswell Air Force Base on Marine One, the President's official helicopter and shown the UFOs (plural) that crashed there and the bodies of their presumably extra-terrestrial pilots. I shook hands with Sasquatch beneath the moonlight under the rotunda of the Jefferson Memorial in Washington DC. I was helicoptered to Greenbrier, the secret underground government bunker where I would be taken in the event of a global thermonuclear war. What were we supposed to do while we were hunkered down in Greenbrier waiting for the radiation to decay down to levels where humans could once again return to the surface of the earth? Greenbrier offered free soft drinks, and free pinball. Considering I was told by my Chiefs of Staff that it would take one thousand years following a global thermonuclear war for radiation to decay to levels where humans could once again return to the earth's surface, I am forced to conclude that's an awful lot of soft drinks and pinball.

$ $ $

Before I was appointed President by Congress, when I was still just a lowly Vice-President, I was told I would be transported to Greenbrier if America ever reached DEFCON 4 (all caps) - a condition of military readiness with (if memory serves) the underpants soiling caption of "Imminent Nuclear War" (or was DEFCON 1 "Imminent Nuclear War?"). There were colors to go along with each armpit dampening lurch forwards towards global thermonuclear war. The end of the world was color-coded. I don't remember what the colors meant. I just remember one of the colors was "blue". Which does not help me remember what "blue" meant in terms of our descent into a global thermonuclear war where the living would envy the dead. And I don't think the color scheme would have helped the American people. If I told you, as President, in a special prime-time emergency address that our chance of being vaporized in a nuclear holocaust in which the living envy the dead was "blue", I think you might be understandably puzzled. I probably should've paid better attention in the meetings with the Joint Chiefs of Staff. But I figured it was information I would need only if I became President. And I figured my chances of becoming President were about as close to zero as was mathematically possible. I assumed me becoming President would involve some sort of post DEFCON 1 (DEFCON 4? Blue? Yellow? Orange? Purple?) scenario. I figured it would involve a "living envying the dead" scenario. And I figured if it was a "living envying the dead" scenario, then the living who were envying the dead would have other things on their minds than puzzling over whether DEFCON 1, DEFCON 4, blue, yellow, green or fucking paisley meant "all clear" or "prepare to see your entire family reduced to cigarette ash in the nano second before your eyes are liquefied and run down your cheeks from the heat blast of a thermonuclear detonation". But becoming Vice President did not involve a nuclear holocaust. It did not even involve one-third of America crashing and bleeding out during an Ebola outbreak. It was not even a post "most of the mega-fauna on the planet choked to death by toxic clouds following an asteroid strike" scenario. It was a post-Trees scenario. Which as far as I can remember, was not covered in the whole DEFCON system.

$ $ $

I do not know where the Trees came from. I was as surprised as anyone when, on the night of my coronation as the King of New York, the Trees sprouted up, clogging our highways, upheaving our railroad lines, turning our airport runways into forests of mature oak, elm, and maple. After the Trees (AT) everyone was more or less stuck wherever they were Before the Trees (BT). America was once again a traverse-less, terrifying wilderness full of hostile Indian tribes, ravenous wild beasts, and outlaws. And Chinese. We sold the Chinese Texas, New Mexico, Nevada, Missouri, Kansas, Oklahoma, Michigan and Wisconsin. So when the Trees took over, the Chinese were trapped in Texas, New

Mexico, Nevada, Missouri, Kansas, Oklahoma, Michigan and Wisconsin. I was trapped in Albany, the former capital of New York State. On the Empire State Plaza, the collection of buildings that make up the state capital. On a hill overlooking the Hudson River to the east. The buildings of the Empire State Plaza are hideous, brutal, concrete, Stalinist. The names of the buildings that compose the complex evoke all the romance of production quotas for Soviet Collective Farms: The Cultural Education Center, The Justice Building, Agency Building Number One, Agency Building Number Two, Agency Building Number Three, and Agency Building Number Four. And The Egg. Where I live.

$ $ $

The Egg: where I live. Where I was crowned King of New York. They claim it looks like an egg. It does not look like an egg. It looks like a scrotum. An enormous concrete ballsack. The ballsack of someone doing a hand stand in the zero gravity of the orbiting Empire State Building or the orbiting Statue of Liberty. Inside the Egg I tap away on my memoir. I believe it is important for significant public figures to write their memoirs: Kings and Presidents. I was both. Technically I may well still be. No messenger pigeon with a note strapped to its skinny pigeon leg has arrived at the Empire State Plaza telling me otherwise. No person has emerged breathless and wild-eyed from the woods to hand me a letter telling me my services as King of New York are no longer required. Those are the two main means of middle-distance communication now that the Trees have destroyed all the telephone and electrical wires: hand delivery and homing pigeon. Everyone scampered the night of my coronation, a year ago, give or take: the night the Trees took over. Understandable. Trees taking over your country in a single night seems like a textbook definition of "force majeure". Now I am alone in Albany with my Irish wolf hounds Romulus and Remus. I have no councilors or sycophants to advise me (I was *so* looking forward to having my very own sycophants!). I have no royal subjects to rule sagely over. If I ever do manage to locate my royal subjects I will decree an immediate inquiry into the efficacy of using smoke signals for all royal correspondence. I believe it is precisely the sort of wise, far seeing thing a monarch would do. An enormous technological advance in a time of great darkness. Like developing Carolingian Miniature Script, or introducing the Napoleonic Code of Law. That's how badly the Trees kneed us in the balls: smoke signals are now a major technological leap forward.

$ $ $

This is a memoir, not a history. I can only tell you what I experienced directly. I am going to type out what I experienced directly. On a manual typewriter I found in the basement of the Cultural Education Center. On a ream of typewriter paper I found in the basement of Agency Building Number Two. There was only one manual typewriter in the basement of the Cultural Education Center. There was only one ream of typewriter paper in the basement of Agency Building Number Two. If the typewriter breaks down, when the paper is all used up, when the typewriter ribbon finally fades to the point of illegibility, that will be the end of my memoir. So I will attempt to be as brief and factual as possible. Because the manual typewriter I found in the basement of the Cultural Education Center has definitely seen better days. And if I had to guess, I would guess those days were probably during the Eisenhower administration. But that is speculation, and I have decided this work will be one of facts, and direct personal experience. Like shaking hands with Sasquatch beneath the moonlight under the rotunda of the Jefferson Memorial in Washington DC. And jacking off for the Kennedys. Dressed as Kaiser Wilhelm II, complete with pickelhaube.

$ $ $

I do not know how long this typewriter ribbon will last. I do not know the difference between a memoir and an autobiography. Other than the fact that "memoir" sounds more impressive than the rather didactic sounding "autobiography". If I had a dictionary I could look it up. Fact:there is not a single dictionary in the library of the Cultural Education Center. Fact: there is not a single style guide in the library of the Cultural Education Center. Fact: I do not know if the plural of "Kennedy" is "Kennedys", "Kennedies", or "Kennedy's". Fact: this typewriter has been ridden hard and put away wet. By some maniac from the Eisenhower administration. How do I know they were a maniac? Fact: the punctuation on the typewriter. The question mark sticks and the exclamation point is worn down to a nub. Whoever used this typewriter before me rained down holy hell on that poor, defenseless question mark and that poor underserving exclamation point. Who wears out the question mark and exclamation point before everything else? (and here I pause to unstick the question mark key). I do not have a dictionary, but for some reason the word "fulmination" comes to mind. The word "screed" pops into my head. Some lifelong body of work of Questions Asked? Questions Answered! But the upper-case letters tend to jam in the ribbon from overuse, so I assume it was QUESTIONS ASKED? QUESTIONS ANSWERED!!! But that is all speculation, on a rapidly ghosting typewriter ribbon. Fact: the dollar symbol on this typewriter is in mint condition.

$ $ $

Fact: we sold most of America to the Chinese, but we sold New York State to the Japanese. The Japanese weren't interested in any part of America that wasn't New York. So we sold them New York. We sold them New York and then we put the Empire

State Building and the Statue of Liberty in space: in orbit, going around and around and around the earth. The Japanese were not impressed that we put the Empire State Building and the Statue of Liberty in space. They figured they had bought the Empire State Building and the Statue of Liberty when they bought New York State. So we gave them the USS Iowa as a sort of consolation prize. The USS Iowa had been used to shell Japan in the Second World War. So now the Japanese are using the USS Iowa to shell Albany and the Empire State Plaza: The Cultural Education Center, The Justice Building, Agency Building One, Agency Building Two, Agency Building Three, Agency Building Four. And The Egg. Where I live. Those who cannot remember the past?

$ $ $

Direct personal experience: I am living in The Egg, in Albany, and getting shelled by the Japanese with the 16-inch guns of the USS Iowa. This is life AT (After Trees). Fact: America was not ended by thermonuclear war, asteroid strike or Ebola outbreak. It was ended by Trees. We spent a great deal of time and mental energy on worst case scenarios. Worst case scenarios like wandering around an incinerated, irradiated America in tattered rags searching abandoned shopping centers for canned goods while dodging gangs of meth-fueled homicidal sodomites. We thought it would be a world of avoiding being raped, tortured, and left for dead by escaped criminals, biker gangs, and bug-eyed survivalists. Turns out that's just Ohio.

If you predicted Ohio would descend into an Old Testament nightmare inhabited primarily by slave gangs of catamites you would have been correct. If I had predicted my life after the apocalypse would include being shelled by the Japanese with the 16-inch guns of the USS Iowa, I would've been correct. I did not predict being shelled by the Japanese with the 16-inch guns of the USS Iowa. As President, I did not single out "Trees" as the greatest threat to the American way of life. Trees destroyed all the things which made modern industrial life at times almost maddeningly predictable: advanced medical science, antibiotics, vaccines, access to potable drinking water. America is now the land of polio, cholera, and children dying slow, lingering deaths after stepping on a rusty nail. The Trees were far more effective than any terrorist attack at sweeping away the gossamer thin protection of the modern globalized, outsourced life. We all instantly became, not by choice, makers. Except nobody in America knew how to make anything above the level of summer camp crafting: birch bark wallets and God's Eyes made with popsicle sticks and discarded yarn. We had long ago lost all the practical skills that made America into America. All those tasks, we figured, was why God made the Chinese.

$ $ $

Whether or not I am still a King or a President or both or neither does not matter anymore to me. I never really wanted to be either. I am a small man with small dreams: to live long enough to finish my memoir, and to demolish the abomination that is the Empire State Plaza. With the help of the Japanese and the 16-inch guns of the USS Iowa. The USS Iowa is cruising up and down the Hudson River with a major frowny face for any sign that anyone is living rent-free in the state they purchased. The USS Iowa is so huge they cannot turn it around in the Hudson River. They can only sail forward and reverse, like a very fat man who is unable to turn around in a bath tub. Which only seems to add to their overall level of white-hot, impotent rage. Any sign of human habitation sends them apoplectic. They have a particular hard-on for campfires. I have learned to use this to my advantage. I am burning car tires in the buildings of the Empire State Plaza. My efforts are part demolition project, part workout routine: hauling tires up twenty flights of stairs in Agency Building Number

One and dousing them with diesel fuel and setting them alight. The timing has to be just right: too early in the evening and the tires burn out before the gun spotters on the USS Iowa can target them. Too late in the evening and they'll catch me up there with the burning tires, frantically taking the stairs back down three at a time to get out of the line of fire. Once I got the hang of it I moved on to Agency Buildings Two, Three, and Four. So far the results are mixed, leaving the concrete buildings looking like four teenagers with bad teeth and horrifying acne, but still very much intact and standing. Still, it's an improvement.

$ $ $

I once was the King of New York. Now I am stuck in Albany, trying desperately to remember the past for my memoir, which I am writing in The Egg. The Egg is divided neatly in half: two separate theaters, their stages back to back in the center of the space, each facing directly away from the other like two men preparing to pace off for a duel. I write my memoir on a manual typewriter on a desk on one stage. I sleep on a folding cot on the other. Making me feel like I'm enacting two separate, Andy Warhol-inspired pieces of open-ended performance art: "Man Sleeping", "Man Writing Memoir". Both for non-existent audiences. Which I feel only adds to the overall authenticity of the project. When not writing or sleeping I walk around the Empire State Plaza looking up at the Trees, dodging bears, wolves and hormonally overcharged stags, hoping something will jog my memory of life BT. But there's a big part of me that doesn't want my memory jogged. Because one of those memories is of losing my big brother Jackson. And another is losing my Uncle Roo. And they are the only two people who ever paid attention to me. And the idea that I am now completely alone in the world, save trees, bears, wolves, stags and the Japanese with white-hot tears of rage running down their faces aboard the USS Iowa is overwhelming. And every time I sit down at my manual typewriter, in The Egg, in Albany, I am reminded of this fact. I am forced to face the reality that at this time, playing whack-a-mole with the 16-inch guns of the now Japanese owned and operated USS Iowa is the main source of human interaction in my life.

$ $ $

I was (am?) America's first dalliance with royalty (Kennedys aside). The Duke of Indianapolis will dispute this, of course, but there's no way to dispute his dispute. For all I know he's just some guy who showed up at the coronation looking for free food and beer. Fact checking, AT, is basically impossible. Everyone, by default, is who they claim to be. Which is why someone showing up at the coronation of the King of New York claiming to be the Duke of Indianapolis is both utterly ridiculous and oddly reassuring at the same time. Why would anyone who was *not* the Duke of Indianapolis claim to be the Duke of Indianapolis? What was I supposed to do, check his driver's license? Besides, to get to Albany from Indianapolis even before the systemic collapse of America he had to cross Ohio, then known as the Land of Meth Fueled Homicidal Sodomites (which, incidentally, I think would look much better on their license plates than "First in Aviation"). I couldn't very well just turn him away. And his timing was impeccable: showing up the day of the night the Trees took over. Did my coronation cause the Trees to take over? It didn't seem, in the eyes of my guests at least, that I was entirely above suspicion. I tried dropping broad hints that the Duke of Indianapolis suddenly appearing out of nowhere that very day might be the *real* cause of our natural disaster, but no one really bought it. After the Trees everyone mostly just wanted to get home. Understandable. Except they did not have canoes. Not a single guest had had the foresight to bring a dog travois. To save him a return journey across the Land of Meth Fueled Sodomites, I lent the

Duke of Indianapolis the official Presidential helicopter: Marine One. Him and all the other guests we could cram safely in the helicopter took off from the roof of The Egg, last-chopper-out-of-Saigon-style. He was supposed to oversee ferrying the other guests to their home towns before returning Marine One to me in Albany (presumably with a full tank of gas? I'm not entirely sure how helicopter borrowing etiquette works). The Duke of Indianapolis did not return Marine One to Albany. Ergo I am stuck in Albany. From the moment I met him, I had a strong, sneaking suspicion the Duke of Indianapolis was an asshole.

$ $ $

I feel like Kings are supposed to be oversized men with oversized ambitions. But I am a small man with small dreams. Literally: I am three foot, eleven and three-quarter inches tall (don't forget the three-quarters of an inch). I am a small man who is (was) heir to one of America's largest fortunes. The Van Kruup family fortune. Which was founded on jerking off. In period costume. Napoleon. Kaiser Wilhelm II. Julius Caesar. Henry VIII. People like me are supposed to have all sort of interesting stories. I have no interesting stories. Correction: I have *one* interesting story: I once jerked off for the Kennedys. Into an empty Coca-cola bottle. Not in period costume (history, as I believe my memoir will prove empirically, is full of missed opportunities). On their estate in Hyannis Port. Where, when they were not forcing me to jerk off into an empty Coca-cola bottle, they sailed and swam and played touch football. Then my big brother Jackson stumbled upon the Kennedys making me jack off into an empty Coca-cola bottle and knocked their heads together like Moe from the Three Stooges. How could you not love a guy like that?

$ $ $

I was America's first experiment with royalty (Kennedys aside). I was crowned King of New York at 21. That was after I was President of the Remaining States of America at 19. I was the youngest President in American history (take *that* JFK!). You might think 21 is young to be writing my memoirs, but those are dog years (President, King of New York, jerking off for the Kennedys). Besides, 21, AT, is considered the new middle-age (footnote: polio, cholera, stepping on a rusty nail).

I hammer away on my memoir on a manual typewriter in The Egg, in Albany. Manual because there is no power (footnote: Trees). If the typewriter I am working on breaks down I am screwed. I could not fix it. Like most Americans, I could not screw in a lightbulb without crossing the threads (footnote: Chinese). I began this memoir because I thought that was something former (current) Kings and Presidents did (do?). But all I can come up with is "I once was the King of New York", like a cheesy Sinatra song. And "I once was the President of the Remaining States of America". Which does not have the same ring as "I once was the King of New York". Still, it does beat "I once was the Duke of Indianapolis" (footnote: Duke of Indianapolis, if, in the astronomically low chance you are reading this, I still want my helicopter back).

$ $ $

When (if) I finish this memoir, I plan on sliding it into the Presidential Biography section of the library in the Cultural Education Center. Right between Martin Van Buren and George Washington. That's where I got the idea for writing this: the library of the Cultural Education Center, staring dumbly at the presidential biographies section and realizing no one would ever publish *my* presidential biography (because "Trees"). But as soon as I began to try to remember all the things that happened to me I realized I did not *want* to remember all the things that happened to me. Because I would have to remember my big brother Jackson. Because all I have of Jackson is memories. Unresolved, confused, conflicting memories (because "big brother").

I want to remember the past. I do not want to remember the past. The past is a non-stop reminder of what I have lost. What I can never recover. You know, Rosebud and all that crap. We are obliged to remember the past. Those who cannot remember the past etc. etc. Which is horse shit. Nothing prepares us *less* for the future than the past. History did not prepare us for Trees. We thought science would save us. We thought rationality would save us. Science did not save us. Rationality did not save us. Do you remember science? Neither do I. I remember my big brother Jackson. Science can suck a lemon.

$ $ $

I do not want to remember the past, but the past has other ideas: Trees. The Trees did not come with a trigger warning. The Trees should have come with a trigger warning. Before I was King of New York I was the Prince of Pennsylvania (in an unofficial capacity). I was Prince of 10,000 acres of trees (lower case) in rural Pennsylvania. Where I lived with my big brother Jackson. Before he decided to live among, and study, and get eaten by, the Kwakiutl. I believed I would live on Pontactico my whole life. I believed Jackson would live on Pontactico *his* whole life. With me. The Kwakiutl had other plans. Pontactico was trees and bears and wolves. Albany is now Trees and bears and wolves (those who cannot remember the past?). I remember America, and jerking off, not necessarily in that order. America is no more. Which has only redoubled my resolve to jerk the Van Kruup family fortune back into existence. Literally: I already have the costumes: Napoleon, Kaiser Wilhelm II, Julius Caesar, Henry VIII. If it was good enough for our founding patriarch, Great-Great-Great-Grandpa Uwe Van Kruup, it's good enough for me. Now all I need is a canoe or dog travois.

$ $ $

I am resolved to recover the Van Kruup family fortune. I will return the Van Kruup family to their former greatness ("greatness" in quotes). By masturbating. In period costume: Napoleon et al. Fuck you, Rosebud. Apologies in advance, what's left of America. But first: memoirs (plural or singular?). You do not have *one* memory. Unless that memory is jerking off for the Kennedys. With a memory of jerking off for the Kennedys you don't really *need* any other memories. It's a show stopper. First rule of showmanship: don't start with your show stopper. First rule of journalism: don't bury your lead. I think I've effectively managed, in an historic, groundbreaking, literary first, to do both simultaneously. Also: the Empire State Building and the Statue of Liberty in space. But before that: rockets. And before that: Pontactico, our 10,000 acre estate in Pennsylvania.

Chapter 2

Call me Ishmael. My real name, Stanley Astor Jazzhands Super-star Galaxy Gramophone Van Kruup III is not the name of some-one to be taken seriously. It is the name of a white rapper with late stage dementia. Put "General" in front of it and you have the name of an overheated genocidal Central African dictator in need of emergency United Nations military intervention. And this is a serious story. About a serious family. With a serious fortune. We are, or at least *were,* the Van Kruups. Of the Penn-sylvania Van Kruups. Because the Pennsylvania Van Kruups were rich. Very rich. Heavy industry, coal mines, railroads and putting garbage in space rich. And masturbation rich. In public. Dressed in period costume: Napoleon, Kaiser Wilhelm II, Julius Caesar, and Henry VIII. And (I'm assuming, custom-made fol-lowing his arrival in America) Abraham Lincoln. Then we lost it all in the Great Funk Crash.

$ $ $

This is a story about America and jerking off. But first: Rockets. A long, long time ago America was rich and strong and free (rel-atively speaking). According to the manual we were the Land of the Free and the Home of the Brave. Actually we were the land of shit and piss and garbage. Everywhere. So we used rockets to put it all into space.

$ $ $

America had been filling up with shit and piss and garbage for years, decades, centuries. Everywhere was car junkyards and toxic waste in leaky 45-gallon drums. America was full up with discarded fast food wrappers and broken appliances. And Americans just kept on shitting and pissing. At some point

America went from a country full up with garbage dumps to a garbage dump with a country located somewhere within it. America transitioned from a country to the world's largest ecological disaster with relative ease. The richer you were, the easier it was. And since my family was the richest of all, for us it was a breeze. The richer you were the further you could get away from all the stink and filth. And since we were the richest of all we got the furthest away of them all without actually leaving the planet's surface (curse you, Rockefellers in the orbiting Empire State Building): 10,000 acres of untouched forest in rural Pennsylvania: Pontactico.

$ $ $

We are, or were, or hope one day to be again, the Van Kruups of Somerset County, Pennsylvania. Those of us that are left, of course. Those of us who haven't been eaten by the Kwakiutl or stepped down the elevator shaft of the Empire State Building or been killed in a freak jet pack accident. Once upon a time you could tell our tax bracket even by how we died. Poor people don't get eaten by the Kwakiutl. Poor people die of emphysema and complications related to diabetes and heart disease. Poor people do not spend their adult lives on permanently airborne, atomic-powered 707 jet airplanes. Which is where Uncle Roo, the uncle who stepped down the elevator shaft in the Empire State Building lived. To the best of my knowledge, poor people do not live on 10,000 acre walled estates in rural Pennsylvania. The Van Kruups lived on a 10,000 acre estate in rural Pennsylvania: Pontactico.

The Kennedys had their compound on Cape Cod. The Roosevelts had Springwood, their mansion and grounds on the Hudson River in Hyde Park, NY. We had Pontactico: 10,000 acres of forest with a thirty foot wall all around it and a castle at its exact center. Sort of. A castle built to the specifications of a masturbating midget (or, if you prefer, "little person"): Great-Great-Great-Grandad Uwe, our family patriarch. A castle shrink-rayed down to hobbit size. Me size. Three foot, eleven and three quarter inches size. A miniature castle in the middle of an enormous estate where I lived in total isolation for the first 19 years of my life. Happy, as far as I could tell. Then Father decided I needed to see more of the outside world. So I saw the outside world. I saw the Kennedys in their compound on Cape Cod. And the Kennedys made me jack off into an empty Coca-cola bottle.

$ $ $

The Kennedys had their compound on Cape Cod where they would gather to engage in all sorts of nauseatingly wholesome pursuits: touch football, sailing, swimming in the bracing waters of the Atlantic Ocean. We had Pontactico: more the sort of place destitute parents in fairy tales would leave their children to get eaten by wolves. Unlike the Kennedys or the Roosevelts or the Rockefellers, the Van Kruups, from day one, seemed to have no urge to present and carefully manage any sort of public profile. For most of our history, the Van Kruups were a vacuum, a spectral presence in the American consciousness, a cipher, a looming sentient cumulus thunderhead flashing heat lightning on the horizon. A financial pillar of smoke and fire ready to bestow its abundance or close down your town's only factory, mine, or rolling mill on an economic downturn, quarter cent drop in the world price of copper, or simple, inscrutable market whim. Before Father ran for President, nobody even knew Pontactico existed. And neither Great-Great-Great-Grandad Uwe Van Kruup or any of his progeny seemed interested in buying the favor of America like the Rockefellers or the Carnegies. There are no Van Kruup art galleries, museums, or public libraries. Uwe went Bobby Fisher - making his millions and then vanishing in a ninja smoke bomb to Pontactico. Where every Van Kruup after him stayed, more or less. Where I planned to stay. Then we lost everything in the Great Funk Crash.

$$\$ \ \$ \ \$$

To be honest, I'm not sure how many Van Kruup hospital wings or Van Kruup collections at the Museum of Modern Art it would've taken for America to overlook Uwe's humble, if singularly honest origins as a public masturbator. In fairness, there is no template for Uwe in the bootstraps mythology America so loves. Jacking off as a source of a vast fortune just doesn't fit the same "Luck and Pluck" formula of an Andrew Carnegie ascending from simple messenger boy to founder of US Steel. And if Horatio Alger ever detailed the rise of a public masturbator to financial royalty in one of his excretory "Risen From the Ranks" novels, there was no copy of it in the library on Pontactico. Then again, Horatio Alger seemed to have a literary blind spot for all the things that *really* went along with rising from the ranks. At least rising to the level of American financial behemoth: price fixing, strike breaking, skull-cracking Pinkerton men and so on. The sort of stuff nobody lists on all those bronze plaques on the sides of all those hospitals, museums, and public libraries. None of the aforementioned offenses, to the best of my knowledge, anyone ever accused Uwe of. Uwe, true to the myth-tradition of the American immigrant, arrived on our shores with a few dollars to his name and a steamer trunk full of period costumes and one simple, take-it-or-leave-it question: "Do you, the American diversion seeking public, wish to see a midget (or if you prefer, "little person") dressed as Napoleon, or the Kaiser Wilhelm II, or Caesar, or Henry VIII (or, later on in his career, Abraham Lincoln) jerking off like it was about to be outlawed?" And if Uwe's swift rise to financial prominence is any indication, America's answer was an enthusiastic "HELL YES!".

$ $ $

Uwe showed up in America with one very important asset (aside from the steamer trunk full of period costumes): his enormous cock. Then he vanished into the wilderness of America. Then, when he'd made enough money, he re-materialized to buy his own *personal* wilderness: Pontactico. From the Pawhtnatawahta Indians. There was oil under the land he bought from the Pawhtnatawahta Indians. Uwe did not share the oil, or the staggering profits derived thereof, with the Pawhtnatawahta Indians. Uwe was learning quickly what it took to make money in America. After diversifying his fortune into coal mines and railroads and steel mills, Uwe vanished into his private wilderness of Pontactico.

Before he hermetically sealed himself inside Pontactico, Uwe toured around his industrial empire in a tricked out rail car: making sure the railroads carried the coal to the coke mills, that the coke mills produced sufficient quality coke for the steel mills, that the iron ore steamships on the Great Lakes were carrying the iron ore to the steel mills and so on. Then, presumably when he had tinkered and toyed with his empire enough so that it achieved a sort of independent gyroscopic stability all its own, he shut himself up inside Pontactico. Where I believe the Van Kruup family underwent some sort of Darwinian speciation event making their survival outside Pontactico, outside the protection of the Van Kruup family fortune, impossible. We vanished from public view and public awareness. Like the Passenger Pigeon. Like the Buffalo. Like the Pawhtnatawahta Indians. But we weren't extinct like the passenger pigeon, the buffalo, or the Pawhtnatawahta Indians. We were just stuck in our tiny evolutionary cul-de-sac. We could no longer live in regular society. We could not live without our fortune. The Van Kruup family fortune had become the Sphinx Moth to our Madagascar Christmas Star Orchid: the pollinator we were completely dependent on because it was the only creature with the requisite foot-long proboscis to reach down into our depths and ensure our continued survival. The Van Kruup family fortune, like Frankenstein's monster, had achieved a peculiar, in our case unintentional, sentience all its own.

$ $ $

One of the goals of the truly rich is to remain truly anonymous. I'm not talking about a few paltry millions here. I'm talking about the sorts of vastly fluid amounts for which there is no real accounting. An amount of money that proves its alchemy *beyond* mere numbers. Fortunes so huge no one person or even group of people can truly be said to be in control of it. Sentient money. Nothing good can come of having your name tagged to that amount of money. Things like your family being sent your severed ear in the mail are the result of people knowing you have that amount of money. The truly rich are truly serious about nobody knowing who they are with the exception of a handful of other truly rich people. A birth notice or a marriage announcement in a single newspaper is considered pushing the edge of decorum. Always stated in the secret, coded short hand of the super rich: the key to the cipher to understand which fortune you stand to inherit, where you went to school to learn the basics of how to groom and tend said fortune, whose fortune you married to your fortune to make one even larger, aggregate fortune, and who stands to inherit that fortune once you've dropped dead. Please note the common denominator in all these punctuating life events: not the person, the fortune.

Uwe may not have cottoned on to the other aspects of public life that go along with being the founder of a vast American industrial fortune, but he took to the anonymous part like a proverbial duck to water. He vanished into Pontactico and was never seen or heard from again by the world outside Pontactico. No marriage notice, no birth notices, only a death notice, in 1926, on the eve of the Great Depression, which was placed in one New York and one Philadelphia paper. Then nothing.

$ $ $

Uwe arrived in America with his enormous cock and a steamer trunk that was more than a steamer trunk. It was a marvel of ingenuity and craftsmanship that could be opened and assembled into various configurations for all the purposes required by a professional jerkoff artist: a stage, a wardrobe, a desk, and even a tiny printing press for producing his own tiny handbills. It contained costumes and scripts for his performances: excerpts from Shakespeare, poems by Longfellow, even a copy of the Gettysburg Address, presumably to go along with his Lincoln costume, which he presumably added after he arrived in America. Uwe's trunk testified that he was no mere back alley, cross-eyed, hairy-palmed, jerkoff geek. Uwe was an *artiste*.

Uwe arrived in America in the decade following the Civil War, to a country eager for distraction from the collective national PTSD of the Civil War and Antietam and Bull Run. Although I have no way of knowing for sure, I imagine Uwe striding confidently into crowds of working men streaming out after their shifts in New England factories running white hot in the post Civil War railroad and industrial boom. Perhaps dressed as Napoleon, swinging his semi-erect penis in slow, lazy circles as a rich man might meditatively swing an expensive pocket watch. Maybe catching the attention of a crowded Cleveland working man's tavern on a busy Friday night dressed as Henry VIII and challenging the patrons to hang items on his rock hard cock: top hats, empty beer growlers, walking sticks and umbrellas. Perhaps even taking bets as each object was added against the point of failure of its structural integrity. Whatever he did, it worked, and he managed, in an astonishingly short time, to amass the nest egg that would allow him to buy a huge swath of land from the Pawhtnatawahta, and then sell the oil from under the land, and then build that money into one of America's largest fortunes. Then Father lost it all in the Great Funk Crash.

$$ $ $ $ $$

Pontactico: one very large financial reservation for one very small, very rich human: me. And my big brother: Jackson. Before he left to live among, and study, and get eaten by the Kwakiutl, a noble race of people living in the Pacific Northwest rainforests of British Columbia, on the west coast of Canada. God I loved my brother. God I hate the Kwakiutl.

I did not see the Kwakiutl eating my brother coming. The future, many painful lessons have taught me, is like that: Trees; The Great Funk Crash; the Chinese buying Texas, New Mexico, Nevada, Missouri, Kansas, Oklahoma, Michigan and Wisconsin. Nobody saw that coming. And Rockets putting our shit and piss and garbage into space.

$$ $ $ $ $$

Actually, we saw the Rockets coming. It was no big surprise that America had run out of places to put its shit and piss and garbage, so putting it all in space seemed like a no-brainer. We had tried everything we could think of to get rid of our garbage. We tried dumping it into volcanoes, but the volcanoes barfed it back up, which meant we ended up with a bunch of burnt shit and garbage. The only thing which smells worse than shit and garbage is burnt shit and garbage, so we stopped putting shit and garbage in the volcanoes. We even sent people to colonize that enormous pile of plastic garbage the size of Texas floating around in the Pacific Ocean. Which, to everyone's amazement, they did. And then to everyone's amazement the island they created out of all the garbage seceded from America and formed the People's Democratic Island Republic of Garbage. And then when we asked them to take our garbage, which was sort of the whole point of creating the island in the first place, they flat out refused. When a place called the People's Democratic Island Republic of Garbage refuses to take your garbage, you know you're in big trouble.

$ $ $

The People's Democratic Island Republic of Garbage (or, as the newspapers came to refer to it, "Garbage Island") wouldn't take our garbage. We didn't really see that one coming either. That was, after all, the entire point of sending people to create Garbage Island: to build a new place to put all our garbage.

"We didn't put all our time and effort and blood and sweat and tears into making our island just so you could dump all your garbage here!" declared the President of the People's Democratic Island Republic of Garbage (or, as it was abbreviated, the PDIRG). Their President was a woman who had spent almost two decades overseeing the armada of floating garbage processing ships and barges that collected, sorted, and compressed the loose, soupy floating garbage in the middle of the Pacific Ocean into buoyant, interlocking plastic blocks of which their enormous island republic was composed. The President's statement was, of course, patently untrue. The entire raison d'etre of Garbage Island was to take America's garbage, but we decided not to put too fine a point on it. Going to war with a place called "Garbage Island" seemed like a proposal with a very low probability of an upside. Adding insult to injury was the fact that a place named Garbage Island, a place composed entirely of discarded take-away containers, worn out tennis balls, and plastic six-pack holders, was a tropical island paradise of orange and avocado groves and pineapple plantations caressed by gentle Pacific trade winds, all of it growing in a nutrient rich soil of sand dredged off the ocean floor mixed with composted seaweed and algae, was nicer than most of America. That was a real kick in the balls for even the most blindly determined American patriot.

$ $ $

The fact that a place called Garbage Island was nicer than most of America was a tough pill to swallow for most Americans. At least the America where poor people lived. And by then America was mostly poor people. Most of whom wanted desperately to emigrate to Garbage Island. Every week the Garbage Island Coast Guard turned back dozens of boats overcrowded with refugees from America. People were sick and tired of being told how great America was, mainly by people for whom America *was* great: rich assholes like me who could afford their own 10,000 acre estates. Everybody else lived in junkyards in houses built of discarded engine blocks or, if they were extremely lucky, metal shipping containers on the banks of the Mississippi River where the only form of aquatic life were radioactive catfish the size of a VW Minibus who routinely swallowed small children and family pets who were foolish enough to wade into the Mississippi past their ankles. There were no jobs. All the jobs had been exported to places that were so astonishingly horrible and unfit for human life that the people who lived there would've seen living in a garbage dump in a house made of discarded engine blocks as a substantial step *up* in life. Places so terrible they would be afraid to even *dream* of living in a metal shipping container on the banks of a river full of radioactive catfish who often dragged small children into the murky depths of the Mississippi screaming and thrashing for their lives as their parents looked on in helpless horror. So America did the only thing it could think of in response to the nightmarish hellscape it had become: it ran a shitload of lotteries.

$ $ $

America started running a shitload of lotteries to provide the slightest glimmer of cruel hope in a country which had collectively shit the bed in spectacular fashion. Then there were the television shows where crews followed around everyone who had won the lotteries to see what they would do with all the money they won, which was almost invariably something grandiose, pointless, and doomed to spectacular implosion.

One man in Wisconsin who had won the lottery created his own demolition derby league. Except instead of old, beat up cars, he used vehicles in mint condition, straight off the factory floor, luxury automobiles: Rolls Royces, Ferraris, and so on. Another guy bought the Houston Astros baseball team and fielded a team of trained chimpanzees, orangutans, and an assortment of other primates in Houston Astros uniforms instead of the baseball players who were already on the team, whom he assigned instead to working the concessions: peanuts, cotton candy, and hot dogs. Then, to improve his television ratings, the guy who started the luxury demolition derby started exclusively hiring Nobel Laureates as drivers. Which people seemed to like, if his ratings were any indication. Every week millions tuned in to watch (for example) a distinguished, gray-haired Nobel Laureate in economics, famous for revolutionizing our understanding of game theory in relation to inflationary price jumps pegged to peak oil fears, savagely and remorselessly T-bone a Bangladeshi magic-realist novelist cherished in her home country for broadening our empathy for, and understanding of, the never ending pains and sorrows of our current human incarnation. If the viewers were really lucky, perhaps following a particularly egregious infraction of the unwritten Smash Up Derby code of conduct (for example a driver's side door collision) two Nobel Laureates might even come to blows. This was uniquely hilarious as it usually consisted of two grown men, well into middle age, whose entire experience of combat consisted of sniping bitchily over footnotes in scholarly papers, flailing ineffectually at each other like two angry toddlers fighting over a coveted sandbox toy as the crowd roared with laughter. Except when the Bangladeshi magic-realist novelist blew her stack. She was a fourth-degree black belt and, being forced to defend herself against a Japanese physicist in a Chrysler New Yorker who felt she had been sandbagging, delivered a devastating axe kick to her assailant's head so powerful his helmet had to be removed with a reciprocating saw.

The chimpanzee baseball team, for its part, had a short lived period of popularity which climaxed (literally) when the orangutan short stop, a former circus performer named "Professor University", learned that if he pulled out his monkey dick and jacked it for all he was worth, the crowd went wild and threw him peanuts, cotton candy, and hot dogs. Then all the other chimpanzee and orangutan Houston Astros realized what was happening and they decided to get in on some of that sweet free peanut, cotton candy, and hot dog action and started jacking it too. Which, after the novelty wore off, quickly shed its appeal, as everyone realized they were spending top dollar to watch eight primates jack off (albeit in Houston Astros uniforms). Attendance and ratings plummeted, and the franchise folded within a month. The Nobel Laureate demolition league outlived the monkey Houston Astros, though just barely, as there was only a select pool to draw their drivers from, so they quickly ran out of participants, and the owner lost everything and had to retire to his original, pre-lottery-winning home, a house made of old engine blocks in Wisconsin, which the bank had generously allowed him to keep when he filed for bankruptcy.

$ $ $

Garbage Island didn't want our garbage, so: Rockets. That was the only successful business Father ever ran: putting our shit and garbage into space. He used rockets he bought on the cheap from NASA who, like the rest of America, had also gone broke. NASA was broke: the National Aeronautics and Space Administration: the guys who had put a man on the moon in one of humankind's greatest technological achievements. Then Father subcontracted them to put all our soiled adult diapers, used kitchen appliances, and worn out furniture into space. If it's true that every genera-tion gets the leader it deserves, then the sixties had JFK - boldly stating that we should commit ourselves to putting a man on the moon. The Greatest Generation had FDR, guiding our nation out of the hysteria of economic collapse and through a global war of unparalleled savagery. We had Father: the President that sold off Texas, New Mexico, Nevada, Missouri, Kansas, Oklahoma, Michigan and Wisconsin to the Chinese, and who stated in *his* inaugural address that America's new goal should be "to put all our shit and piss and garbage in space". And for a while there it looked like it might even work. America mobilized on a wartime scale to get all their shit and piss and garbage to predetermined collection points, and then watched with pride as it all got com-pacted and loaded into rockets and shot into space. Everybody was feeling pretty good about themselves, and feeling that this was maybe the start of a new thing in America. The return of American gumption and know-how and leading the world in freedom. Or at the very least freedom from shit and piss and garbage. Then we discovered a heartbreaking truth: the Chinese were going to mine our space garbage.

$ $ $

But even with Father paying them to use their left over rockets to put our crap in space, NASA was still pretty much a threadbare operation. And having already put a man on the moon, there was really nothing left for them to do that was exciting or dangerous, or at least so technologically advanced that it seemed like magic or science fiction. They thought everybody would get excited about the orbiting space station they built with the money they made from selling Father the rockets, but that consisted mainly of a bunch of nerd scientists hatching sea monkeys or growing beans from seeds in zero gravity. Which turned out to be basically the same as hatching sea monkeys and growing beans from seeds back on earth. In the end, the scientists just sorta looked like a bunch of nerds at space summer camp, so the tax-paying American public wasn't really interested in having their money used to put a bunch of eggheads in space. This left NASA even more broke than before, as before they had at least been able to quietly collect their allotted amount of tax revenue. So they came up with the idea of having a lottery, like everybody else, except theirs was to put some random person into space. Then they could get back to their core competency: putting nerds, and their sea monkeys, and their beans, back in space.

$ $ $

The lottery to put some random person in space proved lucrative beyond NASA's wildest dreams. The scientists at NASA thought this was because America found nerds in space tremendously sexy, and they were even getting ready to put out a special calendar featuring nerds doing things that they perceived as sexy, like feeding and caring for their sea monkeys. But then it gradually came out that the main reason people wanted to go into space was that there was a minuscule chance the capsule would splash down near Garbage Island and they could swim for it and claim amnesty and escape America for the gentle tropical breezes and pineapple plantations of the People's Democratic Island Republic of Garbage.

$ $ $

So NASA had their lottery to put someone in space and then NASA discovered the winner of their lottery was a guy from Cleveland who was one of those super fat people you sometimes see on daytime talk shows who are so huge they can't even make it out of their own homes, let alone get crammed in a space capsule on top of a rocket, so the super fat guy from Cleveland had to sell his ticket to Father and watch on television like everybody else as Father went to the Houston Astrodome on the moon, and the orbiting Empire State Building and the orbiting Statue of Liberty and so on.

The newspapers all carried the story of the super fat guy from Cleveland with a headline that said "TOO FAT TO GO TO THE MOON". It was a simple statement of fact, but people all over the world took it as a rallying cry against a planet on which only people who were really, Really, REALLY good at something got to do it, and get paid tons of money, and the rest of us had to sit around like fried eggs and listen to them drone on and on about hitting home runs on the moon, or how no one understands how tough it is to be rich and famous and beautiful. Then people put "TOO FAT TO GO TO THE MOON" on T-shirts to express the way they felt about their shitty lives in a shitty country on a shitty planet. Kids bought the T-shirt, even skinny kids, to show they had had it to the teeth with their parents, and school, and life in general, and it made them feel a little better about things. Then some famous people wore the T-shirt because they thought it would be ironic and funny, even though that wasn't supposed to be what they were used for, but that's just the sort of assholes celebrities are.

$ $ $

The super fat guy from Cleveland was named Jimmy, and when the asshole news crews found out he was so fat he couldn't even make it out of his house they descended on his home in Ohio and broadcast all sorts of embarrassing and humiliating details about his life. Like how he was so fat he couldn't fit through the front door of his house to go outside. And how he had broken the toilet in his house simply by sitting on it with his enormous weight. And that afterwards he had to have a specially reinforced toilet made especially for him and that all the doors leading to the toilet had to be widened so he could trundle his enormous girth through them without getting stuck, and so on. Then some jackass who had hit a home run in the World Series in the Houston Astrodome on the moon showed up out of nowhere and started yammering on about how touching and inspirational Jimmy's battle with his weight was, and how Jimmy had become a beacon of hope to all Americans, even those who weren't technically American anymore because China had bought their home state. It was all bullshit, of course, but somebody who's done something like hit a home run on the moon will never shut the fuck up about it.

$ $ $

As part of the Space Lottery, NASA built an exact replica of the Apollo rocket that had carried the original astronauts to the moon. They figured that's why so many people bought lottery tickets: they were crazy about the original moon landing. This, of course, was before they discovered the main reason people wanted to go to outer space was in the hope of crash landing on Garbage Island. They thought they needed to sex up the lottery by making the rocket and command module cool and retro. People didn't want cool and retro. They wanted to crash land on Garbage Island. NASA figured they would simply cram whatever random retired school teacher or pimply teenage science fiction buff who won the lottery in the capsule and put them into a few near-earth orbits then plop them back into the ocean and then go back to business as usual: putting scientists and the sea monkeys and bean sprouts back in space. But when they realized they would not even be able to get Jimmy out of his own house because of his enormous size, let alone cram him in a capsule no bigger than a glorified broom closet, they gave Jimmy the option of selling his winning ticket off to the highest bidder. Father was the highest bidder.

$ $ $

Father could outbid everybody for Jimmy's ticket to outer space on account of he was one of the few people in America still filthy rich. Literally: he was the guy who put all of America's busted and out of style crap into space. It all orbited up there like the rings of Saturn. Only instead of being made of rocks and dirt and ice, our rings were made of compacted human excrement, busted television sets, rusted out car mufflers and so on. That was the only industry America had left: putting our shit and piss and garbage in space. Father put all our shit and garbage in space. Father was a garbage tycoon. He was also technically a midget (or if you prefer, "little person"). So when the asshole reporters found out Father had bought Jimmy's ticket to outer space they made fun of Father too, just like they had made fun of Jimmy. They said Father would need a special booster seat in the rocket, and that NASA would have to spend millions to make a special, rocket-friendly booster seat. They made up an info-graphic showing how many of Father it would take, by mass, to equal one Jimmy, and so on. And when they asked Jimmy how he felt about Father buying his ticket, Jimmy whispered softly, almost as if just to himself, slightly beyond the range of the television microphones: "Motherfucker stole my ride." So the reporters kept badgering him to repeat what he had just said, until finally, in frustration, Jimmy screamed terrifyingly, at the tops of his lungs as if in unbearable physical pain: "MOTHERFUCKER STOLE MY RIDE!". And when people heard that they put it on

T-shirts too, mainly to show that they were angry rather than sad about their lives, and how rich assholes owned everything, and poor people were expected to feel lucky if they lived in a house in a junkyard made of greasy, discarded engine blocks. It even crept into use as a common, everyday expression, something "TOO FAT TO GO TO THE MOON" had never done.

$ $ $

I said that history was bullshit, but I was wrong. History can teach us two things. One: Funk, not science or the will of a hairy, angry, possibly insane God is the binding, animating force of the universe. Two: white people have no business messing with the Funk. Funk is not in our nature. The Funk is not in our DNA. Which is not to say that white people don't, from time to time, completely by accident, in a "million monkeys on a million typewriters" sort of way, create some Funk of their own. But by the time I became President of the Remaining States of America the last truly Funky thing white people had done was put a man on the moon. And they had not even intended for that to be Funky. It was one of the only Funky things white people created themselves. They hadn't just stolen it from black people and watered it down for mass consumption. Which really came out of left field for black people, as not a lot of them had much interest in going to outer space. They figured the entire thing was some kind of bizarre running joke cooked up by white people, like ice hockey and country music. It made no sense why anyone would want to pack themselves into a tiny capsule on top of a million pounds of high explosive rocket fuel, then ignite that fuel and go hurtling into space, a place without oxygen where, if something went wrong, you would instantly freeze to death while watching the blood boil in your veins. Jimmy, the super fat guy from Cleveland, was an exception. Jimmy was black, but he wanted to go to space like a motherfucker.

$ $ $

That was the first line of the article with the headline that said "TOO FAT TO GO TO THE MOON!": "Jimmy, as a small boy growing up in Cleveland, always wanted to go to space like a motherfucker." And then the article detailed how when he was growing up he had idolized the astronauts, even though they were almost all white, and how he watched old re-runs of The Six Million Dollar Man constantly, even though technically Steve Austin was a test pilot, not an astronaut. But Jimmy felt that was close enough, as many of the original Apollo program astronauts had started out as test pilots, even though all the original Apollo astronauts had been white. Jimmy was crushed when he realized white people just assumed black people didn't want to go to space. Then years went by, and Jimmy's dream of going to outer space got further and further away, and he started eating to dull the pain and sadness and got fatter and fatter and fatter and pretty soon he couldn't even get out of his house. Then, when he found out he had purchased the winning Space Lottery ticket, the assholes at NASA told him he was too fat to go in the rocket.

"That hurt like a motherfucker," Jimmy said when he heard the news.

$ $ $

Jimmy could say "motherfucker" and the newspapers could print it because mostly nobody gave a fuck about swearing any more. People had bigger problems. Like our entire planet being turned into shit and piss and garbage. And the Chinese mining our space garbage. Half way through my first term as President of the Remaining States of America the newspapers were all printing words like "motherfucker" and "asshole" and "shithead". Newscasters on television were saying things like "The weather this weekend is gonna be shit", and "This just in:

the world is totally fucked" and so on. The real turning point in terms of America-wide everyday use of profanity had come early in my administration when the distinguished, gray haired Nobel Laureate in economics, famous for revolutionizing our understanding of game theory in relation to inflationary price jumps pegged to peak oil fears, savagely and remorselessly T-boned the Bangladeshi magic-realist novelist cherished in her home country for broadening our empathy from, and understanding of, the never ending pains and sorrows of our current human incarnation. Still furious about the hit, which she felt was a cheap shot, she exclaimed in the post derby interview, "Fuck that fucking fucker!". As no one expected a distinguished Nobel Laureate to swear a blue streak, there was no time delay on the broadcast, and it went out live all over America. Before long people started printing T-shirts that said "FUCK THAT FUCK-ING FUCKER", and while it did break down a lot of barriers to people saying "fuck" in everyday conversation, it never really got to be as popular as "TOO FAT TO GO TO THE MOON!" or "MOTHERFUCKER STOLE MY RIDE!".

$ $ $

When we found out the Chinese were going to mine our space garbage, the headlines in the newspapers said things like "MOTHERFUCKING CHINESE TO MINE OUR MOTHER-FUCKING SPACE GARBAGE!". The Chinese sending space ships to outer space to mine our garbage was bad news for Father. Jimmy, the super fat guy from Cleveland, would go on to become a Funk Baron, but at the time Father was still a Garbage Tycoon: Father owned the company that put all our crap into space in the first place.

When Father started his business the garbage was mainly old, worn out stuff, or stuff that had gone painfully out of fashion. Like avocado colored stoves and refrigerators or bald car tires.

But then it became a status symbol for bored rich assholes to put brand new, straight off the factory floor cars, entire suites of brand new kitchen appliances, and Gucci hand bags into space. So when the Chinese saw all that, they figured they'd just go up there and bring it back. They figured we were done with it anyway, otherwise why the fuck would we put it in space? Besides, unlike America, China needed even the raw materials from the garbage we'd compacted into blocks - metal from old car engines, rubber from worn out car tires and so on. America didn't need the raw materials. America made nothing. America's entire economy, as I discovered awkwardly upon consulting with my Treasury Secretary when I took office, the super fat guy from Cleveland named Jimmy, consisted almost entirely of putting garbage in space and watching assholes hit home runs in the Houston Astrodome on the moon. And even those two things weren't exactly going gangbusters. Most people in America were so poor almost everything they owned could've been technically classified as garbage anyway, but they didn't have the money to put it into space. They had to just sit there living with it. Bored rich assholes tried to set a good example by purchasing all sorts of mint condition consumer products and then launching them into space in an attempt to shame poor people into buying more useless crap to keep the economy afloat, but mostly everybody was sick to the teeth of buying useless crap on credit, and wearing that useless crap out, or discovering on television shows that took them inside the million dollar homes of assholes who'd hit a home run on the moon that the useless crap they'd bought on credit was now out of fashion useless crap and that they were supposed to get rid of it and buy new useless crap so their shitty friends and neighbors didn't make fun of them. Then came the Great Funk Crash.

Chapter 3

This is a story about America, and jerking off, and the Van Kruup family, which is me: I am the only surviving Van Kruup (eaten by the Kwakiutl, freak jetpack accident, stepped down the elevator shaft of the Empire State Building). Before Father ran for President and blew our cover, no one knew we existed. Before Father became President and sold Texas, New Mexico, Nevada, Missouri, Kansas, Oklahoma Michigan and Wisconsin to the Chinese, people assumed the Van Kruup line had become barren and childless generations ago. The Van Kruup name existed nowhere. There was no Van Kruup corporation, there were no Van Kruup Libraries, there were no Van Kruup Pavilions of hospitals made possible by generous grants from the Van Kruup Foundation. People assumed we had gone the way of the passenger pigeon and the Pawhtnatawahta: extinct, vanished, existing only in black and white photographs in black and white history books of black and white long ago America.

Father appeared before the American people out of the blue, out of nowhere, and then seemed to be everywhere at once, like a confused time traveler with a slightly wonky time machine. Then, not even finishing the first year of his first term as President, he vanished again. Possibly crushed back down to his component molecules and atoms in the unforgiving vortex of some time travel paradox? Reduced to cosmic background radiation static for violating the temporal laws of the universe while trying to avoid the Holocaust and World War II by killing Baby Hitler? Crushed to death under the feet of an angry brontosaurus in the Jurassic Period? And then he seemed to appear again, again all over the place. Like some sort of post-death Elvis. Father was spotted at the Kennedy compound in Hyannis Port. One person claimed to have seen him getting picked up by a big rig while hitch-hiking just outside Cleveland. And so on. None of the sightings could be verified. So until I receive further notice, I must assume I am the only surviving member of the Van Kruup family, and therefore sole heir to the Van Kruup family fortune.

$ $ $

I am sole heir to the Van Kruup family fortune. I am sole heir to a fortune that at one time was larger than the GDP of some industrialized nations. Then came the Great Funk Crash just a few months after I took over as President of the Remaining States of America. The total value of the Van Kruup family fortune, post Great Funk Crash, currently stands (according to Generally Accepted Accounting Principles) at $367.32 (USD). I am currently heir to a family fortune that, in small bills, could be transported in a brown paper lunch sack.

At last count the Van Kruup family fortune stood at $367.32. A sum small enough to fit in a brown paper lunch sack. When was the last accounting of the Van Kruup family fortune? The last time I looked in the brown paper sack I am carrying the Van Kruup family fortune around in: ones, fives, a few twenties and a single hundred dollar note - Washington, Lincoln, Andrew Jackson and Ben Franklin. But here, in Albany, After Trees, the $367.32 is not worth $367.32. It is worthless. It is worth about the same as the brown paper lunch sack I am carrying it around in. I may as well be carrying around a brown paper lunch sack full of Confederate currency, supermarket coupons offering fifty cents off laundry detergent, or Monopoly money. Because the greenback is no longer the world's reserve currency. The world's reserve currency is currently the Blivit. The Blivit was invented by Jimmy, the super fat guy from Cleveland who was TOO FAT TO GO TO THE MOON. A "blivit" is also the word used to describe ten pounds of shit in a nine-pound bag.

$ $ $

When I became President of the Remaining States of America, one of the first things I did was appoint Jimmy, the super fat guy from Cleveland to be the Secretary of the Treasury. Then Jimmy replaced the greenback, which had been rendered worthless by The Great Funk Crash, with the Blivit, which was not backed by industrial output or projection of military might, but Funk. He designed the notes himself. He put Apollo Creed on the fifty Blivit note. No, not the actor who played Apollo Creed: Apollo Fucking Creed. In fact, that's what it said on the little banner beneath the portrait of Apollo Creed on the fifty Blivit note: "APOLLO FUCKING CREED". The hundred Blivit note was graced by Lando Calrissian. No, not the actor who played Lando Calrissian: Lando Fucking Calrissian. He even created a 1,000 Blivit note. On the 1,000 Blivit note he put Steve Austin, also known as The Six Million Dollar Man (or, as it said on the note itself "THE FUCKING SIX MILLION DOLLAR FUCKING MAN"). Whenever I am down or blue, and wonder if my contribution as President actually meant anything, I pull them out and examine them: the 1,000 Blivit note, the 100 Blivit note, the 10 Blivit note (we never did get around to the five and the one).

Thanks to Jimmy, the super fat guy from Cleveland (and, to spread the credit around, to Apollo Creed, Lando Calrissian and Steve Austin, the Six Million Dollar Man), the Blivit is now the world's reserve currency. A man (or woman) with a pocket full of Blivits can range across the continental United States (at least as far as one can range in a virtually impenetrable forest by means of canoe or dog travois) secure in the knowledge their money is good wherever they go: the parts of what used to be America but which are now owned by the Chinese, the Remaining States of America (assuming they still exist), and the Kingdom of New York (assuming it still exists). You can even buy your own slave army of catamites from the Land of Meth Fueled Homicidal Sodomites (or, if you prefer its BT name, "Ohio") if that's your scene. Because the Blivit, unlike the greenback or the

Yen or the Pound, is backed by Funk. And the Funk is backed by Jimmy, the super fat guy from Cleveland. Jimmy was (is?) a Funk Baron. Jimmy, the super fat guy from Cleveland, for all intents and purposes, *is* the Funk. Ergo, America's currency is backed by a super fat guy from Cleveland. Say what you will, but I think it's an improvement.

$ $ $

America fully intended to buy back the states we sold to the Chinese once we got our Funk back. Footnote: we never got our Funk back. We were convinced putting the Empire State Building and the Statue of Liberty into orbit would get America its Funk back. It did not get our Funk back. And if there is one lesson to be learned from history, and from Jimmy, the guy from Cleveland who was so fat he couldn't make it out of his own house; it's that once your Funk goes, everything goes. Funk, not gravity, dark matter, quantum mechanics or Divine Will, we discovered to our horror, is the great binding, animating force in the universe.

Funk: the indefinable essence of all that is awesome, almost invariably created by black people, and almost invariably stolen by white people and re-purposed to turn vast, illicit profits, like jazz, rock and roll, the written alphabet, the concept of "zero", and (give or take) about eighty percent of the fundamental building blocks of all western thought and philosophy. And Gravitational Amelioration, of course, which was discovered by a female undergraduate at Howard University when she combined non-equilibrium thermodynamics, Derrida's theory of post-structuralism, and Go Go music. Of course nobody believed she had done it, being young, black, and a woman. It also didn't help her credibility that she announced her discovery to the world while wearing a TOO FAT TO GO TO THE MOON T-shirt. So she sold Gravitational Amelioration to the Chinese instead, and the Chinese used it to power their enormous space ships in orbit that mined our space garbage.

$ $ $

This is a story about two Americas: America Before Trees (BT), and America After Trees (AT). Two separate, unrelated realities. Unconnected in any way. BT, we were a nation of Answers, Certainties, Convictions. AT, all our Answers, Certainties, and Convictions ghosted off into the Trees. You will not find any Answers in Albany, in the Cultural Education Center. You will find no Certainties in The Egg. You will find no Convictions in the Justice Building. Conclusion: there are no Answers, Certainties, or Convictions in Albany, on the Empire State Plaza. I do not even have an answer for if there are Answers, Certainties and Convictions anywhere else in America, like a mile up the Mohawk River, in Schenectady, for example. If, in the unlikely event you find this memoir, in the library of the Cultural Education Center, in Albany, crammed between the biographies of Martin Van Buren and George Washington, you will have no idea what I am talking about. Me telling you we were a people composed almost entirely, almost to a molecular level, of Answers, Certainties, and Convictions is like me telling you we could time travel or teleport at will. Or that, in this far away, strange time, there was no such thing as Itsy-Bitsy Bourbon Pissing FDRs.

$ $ $

Yes: a world without the consoling presence of Itsy-Bitsy-Well-Oaked-Tennessee-style-corn-whiskey-pissing 32nd President of the United States Franklin Delano Roosevelts (plural). Unimaginable. Inconceivable. Frankly, a world in which the living would envy the dead. You cannot imagine such a world. Those seeking to protect some shred of their sanity in this AT world choose *not* to conceive of it. Wisely. If you are young, a world without Itsy-Bitsy Bourbon Pissing FDRs does not exist anywhere except history books and memoirs like this. A world that is not completely overgrown in Trees does not exist except in history books. You can grasp it intellectually, just as I tried to grasp there was a world outside Pontactico called "America" before I had to leave Pontactico. I'd seen pictures in some of the comically outdated books from Pontactico's library: books containing grainy black and white pictures with awed captions about things like the wonders of the building of the Eiffel Tower and the opening of the Panama Canal. My knowledge of the world outside Pontactico never broke the color photography barrier. The world outside Pontactico was spooky black and white photographs in spooky black and white books. I may as well have been reading books about sea monsters and satyrs. My ignorance of the world outside Pontactico was consummate. I could not consider myself, even according to the most generic metric, "American". I was a citizen of Pontactico. I was Pontacticoian. Which made the appearance of an Itsy-Bitsy Bourbon Pissing FDR doubly troubling. Because I can remember a time on Pontactico before the existence of Itsy-Bitsy Bourbon Pissing FDRs. And then suddenly, one day, they were just there. I had no idea where they came from. There were no pictures of them in my yellowing books in the library on Pontactico. But that might mean they were simply so common in the world outside Pontactico (that strange monochromatic world known informally to me as "America") that they were simply not worth noting. Or that they existed only on Pontactico. Or that they appeared in America sometime between the opening of the Panama Canal and my discovery of them on Pontactico. And then at some time between the opening of the Panama Canal and present day they had become so routine as to be beneath a spooky black and white picture of them in the books in the library on Pontactico. It was all a guessing game to me, a thought experiment. Like you trying to imagine a world before Itsy-Bitsy Bourbon Pissing FDRs. Or me trying to imagine Pontactico without Macaroni and Cheese Bushes.

$ $ $

Before Father revealed our presence to the outside world by running for President, no one outside Pontactico knew we existed. I'm pretty sure no one cared. They might've cared if they knew Pontactico contained Macaroni and Cheese Bushes and Itsy-Bitsy Bourbon Pissing FDRs, but they did not. And I had no way of knowing that I would be the one to introduce Itsy-Bitsy Bourbon Pissing FDRs and Macaroni and Cheese Bushes into America (the America outside Pontactico, to be technical). And I could not know this until after I had done it, because I did not know the world outside Pontactico did not contain Macaroni and Cheese Bushes and Itsy-Bitsy Bourbon Pissing FDRs.

I'd like to say I was forgotten on Pontactico, but that would infer people knew about me in the first place, which they did not. I cannot even say if anyone knew about Pontactico in the first place, then forgot all about it, like Fordlandia, Henry Ford's bizarre attempt at a corporate mini-state in the rainforests of Brazil. But while Fordlandia was built with a mission (harvesting rubber for the tires of Ford's motor cars) Pontactico seemed to have no purpose beyond isolation and concealment. It is a riddle, wrapped in an enigma, inside 10,000 acres of forest with a thirty foot tall stone wall all the way around. The estate as a whole seems built to be of no standardized scale. It is big. It is small. It is gigantic, and (in the case of the Bourbon Pissing FDRs) it is itsy-bitsy. It is a vast trompe l'oeil. The castle at its center is miniature. Built to the scale of our midget (or, if you prefer, "little person") founder: Uwe Van Kruup. It is Me-sized. All of it shrunk down, proportionally speaking, to snow globe size by the 10,000 acres of forest around it. With the Youghiogheny River running right through it. The Youghiogheny River is traversed by a one-third scale exact replica of the Rialto Bridge in Venice. And on the other side of the river, accessible only by the one-third scale Rialto Bridge, is Tiny Town.

Tiny Town, as its name implies, was built for Tiny People (or, if you prefer, "midgets"): the tiny servants who looked after Uwe in his tiny castle. Tiny Town was not always tiny, and it was not always on Pontactico. Once upon a time it was a Regular Sized Town with Regular Sized People with a Regular Sized Name: Frenchmans Bend. It was (I assume) originally full of Regular Sized People doing their Regular Sized Jobs. Then Uwe bought 10,000 acres in rural Pennsylvania, on which the regular sized town of Frenchmans Bend stood, so Frenchmans Bend (or, more accurately the entire human population of Frenchmans Bend) had to go. Then the road which ran through it had to be relocated. Eventually the re-routed road became part of the interstate highway system, which ever thereafter followed a broad deferential arc around Pontactico like a beam of light being warped by its passage near a black hole. Then Uwe willed a strange transformation of the town itself. The town of Frenchmans Bend was cut down to size. Literally: the entire town was scaled down to little person size by cutting a procrustean one third vertical slice out of every building, leaving all its horizontal dimensions intact, giving it a squat, hunkered down appearance. Which is where the small army of little person servants who looked after their little person master lived. At least until some time between the founding of Pontactico and the beginnings of my memory. Me and Jackson didn't need an army of servants: we had Macaroni and Cheese Bushes.

Great-Great-Great-Grandad Uwe's miniature castle was flanked by a menagerie on one side, and a library on the other. Me and Jackson lived in the library. Because the library was normal size, but the castle was miniature. Jackson was normal size. To make his way around the miniature castle would have required him scuttling about bent at the waist or on his knees like a Victorian tin miner working a seam. So he stayed mainly in the library. We were not supposed to go in the menagerie. We were not supposed to go to Tiny Town. This was never made explicit. It was just sort of understood. Like it was understood we weren't supposed to leave Pontactico. The menagerie could only be reached through a set of solid oak doors. The doors were locked (clue number one we weren't supposed to go in the menagerie). The windows of the menagerie were boarded up (another subtle hint). Tiny Town was accessible only by the one-third scale Rialto Bridge, which was the only bridge across the Youghiogheny River. The bridge was blocked by a heavy iron gate. The gate was locked. Except for once a year, on Thanksgiving - the only day Father came to visit us, together with his brothers: my Uncle Roo and my Uncle Dash. Then Father would unlock the gate and they would all cross over to the other side of the Youghiogheny River, to Tiny Town, to discuss family business. And they would take Jackson with them, but not me. Which naturally steamed me to no end. So I naturally had to see what was on the other side of the one-third scale Rialto Bridge. And what I saw was Tiny Town.

I had no idea what to expect on the other side of the river. I did not expect to find Tiny Town, seemingly stopped in time, as if all the inhabitants had decamped en masse, without sufficient time to take anything but the clothes on their backs. They had left behind everything, as if they had been awoken in the middle of the night and been given fifteen minutes to get out of the oncoming path of some looming cataclysm or natural disaster, a tornado or a burst dam upriver. Or a tiny hydrogen bomb had been detonated directly over Tiny Town, vaporizing everyone who lived there, but leaving all their personal effects and belongings intact, in situ: long ago discontinued brands of soap, toothpaste, tinned beef, and candy. Their spooky black and white photographs still hung on their walls: tiny first communions, tiny family portraits, tiny candid snapshots at church picnics and Fourth of July pie-eating contests (complete with tiny pies, of course). None of which really explained to me why Father, Jackson, and my Uncle Roo and Uncle Dash would go there every Thanksgiving.

$ $ $

Pontactico seemed frozen in time. But what that time was I really have no idea. Nothing in Pontactico pointed to any particular year, or even era. It seemed outside of any time, yet part of all of them, if that makes any sense. Tiny Town, judging from all the expired consumer products, had been a thriving place *some* time in the past, but when the consumer goods had expired, and from what era, was impossible for me to determine. The rest of Pontactico felt like a stage set for how someone in the future would imagine the past, if that person had scored poorly in standardized testing in history. All the books in the library were from the past. All the samples in the menagerie where from the past. But why someone had assembled the contents of the menagerie or to what purpose, if any, was a real head scratcher. Unless that purpose was to permanently fuck up me and Jackson's lives. Because inside the library and inside the menagerie respectively, were the two things which would determine the course of our lives almost beyond everything else: a rare, intact, 20 volume set of Edward Curtis's haunting work "The North American Indian" (to be exact, volume 10 of "The North American Indian": the Kwakiutl); and a naked pickled, Pawhtnatawahta woman. But first: the Itsy-Bitsy Bourbon Pissing FDRs.

$ $ $

Yes: Itsy-Bitsy Bourbon Pissing FDRs. But first: the menagerie. Which, by rights, is where I should've found the first Itsy-Bitsy Bourbon Pissing FDR. Instead, I found him floating face down in the Youghiogheny River, exact and perfect in every itsy-bitsy detail, minus one shoe, with the striped trousers of his morning suit around his ankles as if he'd just stepped off a black and white newsreel of his inauguration (if FDR had been sworn in wearing one shoe and with his pants around his ankles. Historical footnote: FDR did not get sworn in wearing one shoe and with his pants around his ankles (if the books in the library of the Cultural Education Center here on the Empire State Plaza, in Albany are to be believed)).

In lieu of any actual parenting, everything I needed to know about life I learned from the menagerie: that (all idiotic lip service aside) being different, deviating defiantly from the norm, is always a liability. That life is not kind to those who are too big, or too small, or too big in the wrong place, or with the right thing in the wrong place, or the wrong thing in the wrong place. If you are too big, or too small, or just plain too wrong, you can be bought and sold on the open market. That beyond a certain event horizon of normalcy you can be bought and sold and displayed for profit: in a sideshow, in a cabinet of curiosities, in a human zoo, and in a menagerie. Example: Roloff, the Stuffed Russian Lobster Boy - the boy with lobster claws where his hands should be. Career options if you have lobster claws where your hands should be: a sideshow, a cabinet of curiosities, a human zoo, a menagerie. Where, once you have exhausted your drawing power by dying, you can be taxidermied: skinned, gutted, and stuffed like a sofa cushion, and sold to a private collector for their private amusement and diversion. If you are deemed too big, or too small, or too wrong, not even your mortal remains belong to you (exhibit B: the skeleton of John Murphy (aka "The Hannibal Colossus"): cleaned, bleached, and gleaming white in its colossal display case. You cannot be sure that even after your death you will not be ogled and gawked at. And here I must confess to both ogling and gawking: at the naked, pickled Pawhtna-tawahta woman floating Ophelia-like in her enormous, phone booth sized tank of formaldehyde fluid in the menagerie.

$ $ $

Let the record show I both ogled and gawked. She was my first sexual experience. That is to say she was the first person to make me aware that I had the capacity for a sexual experience. So I gawked. I ogled. Then I did something else which I would later become famous for, while wearing period costume (Napoleon, Kaiser Wilhelm II, Julius Caesar, Henry VIII, Abraham Lincoln). Which I won't make you picture. Which I guess I just did make you picture, by saying not to picture it. I was shocked by my response to the naked, pickled Pawhtnatawahta woman. At least as shocked as I could be without the knowledge that my response to the naked, pickled Pawhtnatawahta woman was maybe not the typical response to seeing a naked, pickled, Pawhtnatawahta woman. Or maybe more accurately, the "correct" response. But I did not know this reaction was incorrect. I still cannot say for sure that it was incorrect *for me*. Which forces me to consider a thought experiment of sorts: did stumbling upon the naked, pickled Pawhtnatawahta woman as my first sexual awakening *cause* me to become hardwired to being turned on only by naked, pickled Pawhtnatawahta women (I know it sounds strange using the plural, but stay with me). Was I, inadvertently, in that moment, ruined forever for a satisfying, heteronormative, once a week in missionary position sex life? If I had not discovered the naked, pickled Pawhtnatawahta woman in the menagerie, would the rest of my life (sexually speaking, at least) have been one dull, aching longing for something I could not identify? Statistically speaking, the odds of being pre-wired to be turned on by a naked, pickled Pawhtnatawahta woman, and then actually finding a naked, pickled Pawhtnatawahta woman in my home, in the menagerie, has to be astronomically low. But that doesn't in any way shape or form necessarily rule out that scenario entirely. But without some way to travel back in time to run an alternate scenario, there's no way to know for sure. And while I recognize that this line of questioning is ultimately futile because I do *not* have some way to time travel (in which case, anyway, I'd be too busy trying to track down and kill Baby Hitler) I believe I can state, purely from a personal bias, that I'm glad I didn't stumble upon the Itsy-Bitsy Bourbon Pissing FDR with his pants around his ankles first.

$ $ $

But back to the Itsy-Bitsy Bourbon Pissing FDR: beyond the merely mind bending part of finding an Itsy-Bitsy Bourbon Pissing FDR doing a dead man's float in the Youghiogheny River, was the feeling that, minus his top hat and one shoe and with his pants around his ankles, his state seemed undignified and humiliated. Like a mental patient or prisoner having had their shoelaces and belt taken from them. It made him look like the victim of a prison gang-rape or someone at the end of a particularly horrifying week-long bender. I did find other things floating in the river. Usually dead fish, belly up, their shiny white bellies glowing like a beacon in the dark water. Which was about as close as I could get to identifying what he was at first glance. And here's where the whole "not having anything *not* normal" rubric asserted itself: since I had never seen an action-figure sized dead 32nd President before, I did not know what to make of the tiny figure which floated before me, bobbing and knocking against the sticks, leaves and debris of the Youghiogheny River, as if he'd just traversed the river like someone swimming the English Channel but whom the sheer effort of the endeavor had left utterly exhausted and unable to summon the strength to even haul himself out of the water without assistance.

He was face down. If I had seen his itsy-bitsy face first I might've reacted differently. Instead, the shock of picking him up, turning him over, and finding myself face-to-face with the tiny, hideously bloated face of the New Deal savior of American Democracy, puffed-lipped mouth pulled back in a hideous sneer, trademark cigarette holder still clamped resolutely in his tiny teeth, realizing I was holding a dead human being (admittedly a dead itsy-bitsy human being) made me inadvertently fling him away from me, as if I'd just picked up a stinging insect or poisonous frog. I flung him away, and Itsy-Bitsy Bourbon Pissing FDR described an almost perfect arc, like he'd just been shot out an itsy-bitsy cannon at an itsy-bitsy state fair, and landed squarely on his face on a lily pad in the river. Where he lay perfectly motionless until Romulus, who was padding along, belly deep in the river close by, thinking I had initiated a game of fetch, galloped into the water, clamped Itsy-Bitsy Bourbon Pissing FDR firmly in his enormous jaws and returned to me with said 32nd President, dropping him at my feet and waiting with eager dog expression for me to continue our game.

For a moment I stood there, with the Itsy-Bitsy Bourbon Pissing FDR at my feet, unable to process what was happening in real time, as if my brain was searching frantically for the right conceptual pigeon hole to slot an Itsy-Bitsy Bourbon Pissing FDR into. There was no pigeon hole to slot the Isty-Bitsy Bourbon Pissing FDR into. Should I have dug him an itsy-bitsy grave with itsy-bitsy engraved marble headstone? Possibly. But I didn't bury him. If I had found a full sized human being floating face down in the Youghiogheny River with one shoe and their pants around their ankles, I would've buried them. Which I guess makes me no different than whoever stocked the menagerie with the stuffed, skeletonized, pickled bodies of the too big, the too small, the too wrong, and those with lobster claws where their hands should be. And to be truthful, I was no different from whoever had stocked the menagerie. Whoever had felt comfortable committing such gross indignities on the mortal remains of its inhabitants. Because, after a brief moment of reflection, during which at no time did I consider burying Itsy-Bitsy FDR in an itsy-bitsy grave, I took the Itsy-Bitsy Bourbon Pissing FDR and put him in the menagerie with the too big, the too small, the too wrong, and the naked, pickled Pawhtnatawahta woman.

The first time I saw an Itsy-Bitsy Bourbon Pissing FDR was also the first time I saw a dead person (albeit an itsy-bitsy dead person). I didn't count the dead people in the menagerie. I didn't think of them as dead as much as frozen in some temporary, interstitial state. Definitely not alive, but not wholly dead either. Like a photograph of someone from the past who is now long dead, or an insect trapped in amber. If this was a rationalization to protect myself from the fact that the nexus of my sexual attraction was not merely a "naked, pickled, Pawhtnatawahta woman", but "dead, naked, pickled Pawhtnatawahta woman", I can only leave the answer in the hands of future historians and psychologists (and God help them when they find my memoirs in the basement of the Cultural Education Center sandwiched unassumingly between the biographies of Van Buren and George Washington). Besides, as I said before, it is my opinion there is nothing to be learned from history. Except maybe, if you can help it, don't let your first sexual experience be with a dead, naked, pickled, Pawhtnatawahta woman.

I put the Itsy-Bitsy Bourbon Pissing FDR in the menagerie, with the dead, naked, pickled Pawhtnatawahta woman. Literally: I put him in the tank of preservative fluid with her. I didn't know where else to put him. I couldn't cram him in one of the bottles with one of the fetal pigs. I couldn't put him in one of the bottles with one of the fetal humans. I guess my impulses were similar to whoever had put all those weird things in all those jars of weird, piss-yellow preservative fluids: I had discovered something rare and unique, and was loathe to give it up. I had no way of knowing if I would find more. At the time, I didn't even know he could piss straight bourbon. I didn't know there would be more: both more Itsy-Bitsy Bourbon Pissing FDRs, but (as we all now know, of course) Itsy-Bitsy Gin Pissing Sir Winston Chur-chills, Itsy-Bitsy Peppermint Schnapps Pissing Adolph Hitlers, and Itsy-Bitsy Vodka Pissing Joseph Stalins. I had to work with the information to hand, which implied my itsy-bitsy bourbon pissing Knickerbocker should be somehow saved for posterity. Why I put him in the tank with the dead, naked, pickled Pawht-natawahta woman I cannot say. A brain cramp maybe. Because now I was faced with one of two equally unpalatable options: jerking off to a dead, naked, pickled, Pawhtnatawahta woman *and* an Itsy-Bitsy Bourbon Pissing FDR, or somehow fishing the Itsy-Bitsy Bourbon Pissing FDR out of the tank. Luckily for me, seeing the dead, naked, pickled Pawhtnatawahta woman and the dead, naked-from-the-waist-down Itsy-Bitsy Bourbon Piss-ing FDR together did not key off some new, hitherto undiscov-ered and (thankfully) undreamed of new turn-on: only being able to achieve climax while jerking off to a dead, naked, pick-led, Pawhtnatawahta woman while an Itsy-Bitsy Bourbon Piss-ing FDR floated there with her, suspended in the zero-gravity of the fluid like an itsy-bitsy astronaut on an itsy-bitsy space walk.

Thankfully this was not the case. And it's not like the pres-ence of the Itsy-Bitsy Bourbon Pissing FDR was going to put me off jerking it to the dead, naked, pickled Pawhtnatawahta wom-an. I do not know why I put him in the tank, and I do not know why, faced with the situation, I simply didn't fish him out and put him somewhere else. So maybe I *was* somehow turned on by jacking off to a dead, naked, pickled, Pawhtnatawahta wom-an while an Itsy-Bitsy Bourbon Pissing FDR floated there with her. Or maybe I was just still in a daze over discovering my big brother Jackson, my hero, my idol, fucking a 150-year-old sofa cushion.

Chapter 4

This is a story about America, and the Van Kruups, and jerking off, and Itsy-Bitsy Bourbon Pissing FDRs (plural). And a dead, naked, pickled, Pawhtnatawahta woman. And the Kwakiutl. And my big brother Jackson fucking a 150-year-old sofa cushion. It is a memoir. By a former President. Of a former America. Memoirs written by people who occupy the inner circles of power are supposed to be full of secrets. This memoir has zero secrets. Because I cannot keep a secret. Case in point: me telling you about my brother fucking a 150-year-old sofa cushion. Case in point: me telling you about jacking off to a dead, naked, pickled, Pawhtnatawahta woman. Because I never learned to keep a secret. Because there was no one to keep a secret from. My life was Pontactico, and Pontactico was me, my big brother Jackson, and my Irish wolf hounds, Romulus and Remus. So I knew Jackson had fucked a 150-year-old sofa cushion, and since he caught me watching him, he knew I knew he had fucked a 150-year-old sofa cushion, and by simple syllogism I knew *he* knew he had fucked a 150-year-old sofa cushion, and with that the circle of secrecy was closed. When I became President I instituted a policy of brutal, unflinching truth when communicating with the American people. I told the American public that America was broke. I told the American people about my big brother fucking a 150-year-old sofa cushion. I told the American people about me jacking off to a dead, naked, pickled Pawhtnatawahta woman. I found out one important fact about the American people: they have, at best, a limited appetite for brutal, unflinching truth.

$ $ $

I told the American people other secrets. I told them about the UFOs I had seen at Roswell. I told them America was broke. I told them the greenback had lost its respected position as the world's reserve currency. That the greenback had become worthless. I told them we were scrapping the greenback and instituting a new form of currency, called a "Blivit", which is a word that means "ten pounds of shit in a nine pound bag". This new currency would not feature portraits of Washington, Jefferson, or Ben Franklin. It would have portraits of Lando Calrissian, Steve Austin, and Apollo Creed. I explained to the American People that this new currency, featuring a science fiction bounty hunter, a television character with a bionic eye, arm and legs, and a movie boxer was not backed by industrial might or ability to project military power, but by The Funk, and The Funk was backed by a super fat guy from Cleveland. I thought the American people would respect my brutal, unflinching honesty. Like FDR (the full sized one, not the itsy-bitsy bourbon pissing one). I was wrong. I was no FDR. Not even an itsy-bitsy bit. But I did share one thing with FDR, and Abraham Lincoln, and George Washington: I was a wartime president. I had to summon all the strength and wisdom I possessed to lead America through the crucible of international conflict. Because I was president during the Basketball War.

$ $ $

Brutal, unflinching honesty: we did not sell New York to the Japanese. We lost it to them in a game of basketball. There was a time in America when that sentence made sense. That time was my first term as President of the Remaining States of America. It seemed like a good idea at the time: double or nothing, erasing our debts to Japan if we won. We owed the Japanese almost as much as we owed to the Chinese. We felt confident that we could still, despite all our other problems, beat Japan in a game of basketball and therefore would not have to sell them vast tracts of America at bargain basement prices. Brutal, unflinching honesty: our confidence was greatly misplaced.

America could no longer project any effective military power. We no longer controlled the world's reserve currency. But we felt pretty confident we could at least kick Japan's ass at basketball. America still had all the best basketball players at least. Or, to put it more accurately, we had their brains. Literally: we had the brains of Michael Jordan, Magic Johnson, Wilt Chamberlain and a bunch of others. We had lost Larry Bird's brain somewhere along the line. The loss had involved a drunken post championship victory by the Boston Celtics. They were pretty sure the last time they had seen it was in a cab on their way to a club. And there the trail ran cold. But we had all the other brains. And we had bionics. Just like in The Six Million Dollar Man. Only for real. So we put the brains in new bodies and then made the new bodies bionic, without telling the Japanese. Everyone on our team, in addition to having an unparalleled talent in, and understanding of the game of basketball could jump thirty feet in the air, straight up, flat footed from a standing position and could run the hundred meter dash in two and a half seconds. On the breakout they passed the ball so fast it broke the sound barrier and made a little sonic boom. Then, just as we were about to play the Japanese, somebody found Larry Bird's brain. Or rather, it was produced from a private collection in the midwest under terms of anonymity and general amnesty. None of which we shared with the Japanese.

I think calling it "The Basketball War" was, to be honest, in poor taste. Because Japan and America had fought an actual war just a few generations back, and hundreds of thousands of human beings had been killed. It was supposed to be called "The Sino-American Basketball Challenge in the Interest of International Friendship and Co-operation". But once the assholes in the news got ahold of it, they would start calling it "The Basketball War" and working everyone up into a lather about how America and Japan were "Going to War!" and saying things like the date of the game would "Live in Infamy!". And even though no one was old enough to have actually fought in the Second World War, or even know of anyone who had actually fought Japan in the Second World War, everybody got all hyped up over it. Including the Japanese. Who became terrified at all the bombast and equipped their team with robotic exoskeletons and laser gatling guns and mowed down the American Team in a surprise attack just seconds before the opening buzzer. The Japanese mopped the floor with us. Literally: our entire team was just bits and pieces on the basketball court when they were done with us. Apparently the Japanese had taken the whole "Basketball War" thing literally. Which, in retrospect was surprising, as they didn't seem bothered by the fact that "Sino" meant "Chinese" and not "Japanese", but "Basketball War" had scared the pants off them.

The Basketball War almost caused a real war. But then we remembered we were incapable of projecting military power. We did not even have the biggest battle ship in the world any more: we had sold the USS Iowa to Japan. And we did not know what to do with all the bits and pieces of the Bionic USA Basketball Team. We managed to salvage most of the brains, but the bionic bits and pieces were beyond repair. Everyone who was at the game got a medal, and were honored at the Basketball War Memorial on the moon in a solemn, tasteful ceremony. After which there was a monster truck rally in the Houston Astrodome on the moon. Larry Bird's brain drove one of the monster trucks. Which made everyone wistful and sentimental. Even though no one was entirely sure what they were being wistful and sentimental about, as Larry Bird's brain had never before, to the best of anyone's knowledge anyway, driven a monster truck. It was just a very emotional situation for everyone involved.

Historically speaking, a good war can raise a President's approval rating and political capital. The Basketball War was not a good war. For starters, there was no clear victor. There wasn't even a clear ending. So we refused to hand over New York State to them. Technically, we may still be at war with them. Which would definitely explain the USS Iowa shelling me on the Empire State Plaza from the Hudson River. Which means, technically, I am still a wartime President. But I cannot tell you if it has boosted my approval rating. Since there is no one in Albany to approve or disapprove of me other than my Irish wolf hounds, Romulus and Remus.

I feel I can state with confidence that my approval rating with Romulus and Remus has never been higher. I feel I can state with confidence this approval is due mainly to the fact that I know how to use a can opener, a feat of know-how that is greeted with raised ears and laser-like stares of anticipation every time I open a can of dog food for them. Once or twice a week I scavenge dog food for them from the abandoned supermarkets of Albany. The cans of dog food are heavy. So I transport them back to the Empire State Plaza and The Egg with the only practical means of transportation at my disposal: dog travois. My personal dietary needs can be met without leaving the safety of The Empire State Plaza: grape soda to mix with the bourbon from the Itsy-Bitsy Bourbon Pissing FDR I have brought with me from Pontactico, and macaroni and cheese, from the macaroni and cheese bushes that grow wild on The Empire State Plaza from between the cracks in the great, heaved up concrete paving stones. I did not bring the macaroni and cheese bushes with me from Pontactico. They brought themselves. Technically, they are an invasive species. Like kudzu, cane toads, and zebra mussels. Technically, the Itsy-Bitsy Bourbon Pissing FDRs that live in feral colonies on the Empire State Plaza are an invasive species. Except they don't clog municipal water intake pipes or collapse power lines under their weight. But they will piss an amazingly exact stream of delicious, well-oaked, Kentucky-style corn whiskey with uncanny accuracy into your eye if you happen to catch one. It is their one and only means of self-defense. It is an effective means of self-defense. If you don't believe me, no one has ever pissed delicious, well-oaked, Kentucky-style corn whiskey directly into your eye.

I did not bring the macaroni and cheese bushes with me from Pontactico. I brought my Itsy-Bitsy Bourbon Pissing FDR with me from Pontactico. But I needn't have. Today, AT, Itsy-Bitsy Bourbon Pissing FDRs are everywhere. It's one of the consolation prizes for living in this verdant dystopia. Along with macaroni and cheese bushes. No one, AT, need fear going hungry. As long as they don't mind eating macaroni and cheese for breakfast, lunch, and dinner. Also, no one, AT, need fear being sober. As long as they don't mind drinking delicious, well-oaked, Kentucky-style corn whiskey pissed out by an Itsy-Bitsy New Deal President. The Itsy-Bitsy Bourbon Pissing FDRs have multiplied and thrived, like any self-respecting invasive species. Like most invasive species they have gleefully exploited almost every newfound ecological niche: woodland, swamp, desert, Agency Building Number 2, the abandoned shopping mall in Albany where I scavenge for dog food. The feral Itsy-Bitsy FDRs are like an itsy-bitsy walking, bourbon-pissing alternate history. An alternate history in which FDR is shrunk down to itsy-bitsy, and lives clothed in rags and discarded pieces of plastic, copper wire and elastic bands with a mouth full of itsy-bitsy rotten feral teeth.

The Itsy-Bitsy Bourbon Pissing FDRs have exploited every possible ecological niche, something the Van Kruups could not do. We had one niche, and one niche only: Pontactico. And the Empire State Plaza. So technically, me and the Isty-Bitsy Bourbon Pissing FDRs are currently competing to exploit the same ecological niche. Or rather, I am *attempting* to compete to exploit the same ecological niche. Because I am not sure how much longer I can keep this up. I feel like an exhibit in a natural history museum: the last of the Van Kruups. Next to Martha, the last passenger pigeon. Only Martha was not the last passenger pigeon. Because AT, passenger pigeons are everywhere. Or perhaps more accurately: passenger pigeons are EVERYWHERE! They have returned with a vengeance with the restoration of their ecological niche: Trees. They have returned in swarms. In clouds. Clouds that black out the sun. In biblical masses that block out the sun and seem to demand the redress of some injustice that has found displeasure in the eyes of the Lord against his chosen people. They crowd on Trees and break the limbs of two-hundred-year-old oaks. And everywhere they go they leave mountains of Passenger Pigeon Shit (all caps). Stinking, acrid, knee-deep Passenger Pigeon Shit.

Passenger pigeons are one of the worst things that can happen to a town, a village, or the Empire State Plaza, in Albany. Because I have reason to believe they may be headed for the Empire State Plaza in Albany. Because there are so many of them, technically they must be headed for everywhere. And buffalo: herds of buffalo in numbers beyond reckoning. Descending on your town, your village, your Empire State Plaza in Albany like a snorting, enraged, out-of-control hairy shit-storm. Glaciers are also making a comeback. A slow comeback. A (dare I say) "glacial" comeback, but coming back nonetheless. Because all the Trees are sucking all the carbon out of the air and reversing global warming. Reversing it to the point of "glaciers". I think I am safe from buffalo. I cannot see any buffalo from my lookout on the top of Agency Building Number 3. Or rather, I cannot see the end-of-the-world cloud their numbers throw up when they move. From my lookout on top of Agency Building Number 3 I can see passenger pigeons, far away, maybe toward Pennsylvania. From my lookout on top of Agency Building Number 3 I cannot see glaciers. But I keep an eye out. I figure I know their line of attack. I am keeping a close eye on Canada. Turns out we should not have been worrying about terrorist attack and asteroid strike and thermo-nuclear war. We should have been worried about passenger pigeons. And buffalo. And Canada.

The buffalo are back, which is good news for the Teton Sioux, the Yanktonai, and the Plains Assiniboin (vol. 3, Edward Curtis, "The North American Indian"). Natural abundance is everywhere now: Trees, buffalo, passenger pigeons. We have natural abundance up the wazoo. And glaciers. The appearance of all those Trees, in a single night, have reversed the effects of global warming in an instant. They so reversed global warming that "glaciers". Winter is coming early to the Empire State Plaza. Winter may be coming permanently to the Empire State Plaza. The leaves are showing their brilliant autumn colors in late May. Fourth of July celebrations this year may well consist of fireworks and a light dusting of snow. I cannot see the glaciers coming down from Canada, but I can feel them: in the change of the air from balmy summer to outflow from an industrial grade air conditioner. I will have to keep my eyes peeled, from the top of Agency Building Number 3. Because Agency Building Number 1 has been shelled almost to collapse by the 16-inch guns of the USS Iowa. Because Agency Building Number 2 has been overrun by Itsy-Bitsy Bourbon Pissing FDRs. Now is the winter of our discontent. Or, at the very least, the winter of Trees, glaciers, passenger pigeons, buffalo, and feral Itsy-Bitsy Bourbon Pissing FDRs.

Human history is one giant blind spot. The future of humanity is one giant blind spot. We did not see Trees, glaciers, passenger pigeons and buffalo coming. The Teton Sioux, the Yanktonai, the Plains Assiniboin (volume 3, Edward Curtis, "The North American Indian") did not see the White Man coming (small pox, repeating rifles, land theft, exterminating the passenger pigeon and the buffalo). The White Man thought they saw the end of the North American Indian. Edward Curtis put together "The North American Indian" because he figured in a generation there would be no more North American Indians. He figured The North American Indian was going the way of the passenger pigeon and the buffalo. Edward Curtis believed The North American Indian would be a footnote, and that the only record of their existence would be his 20 volume set, "The North American Indian". Turns out we are the footnote (and by "we" I mean The North American White Man.) Because the Kwakiutl, in their misty, mossy home in the Pacific Northwest, are doing just fine. Because the Teton Sioux, the Yanktonai, and the Plains Assiniboin, with a prairie teeming with buffalo, are doing just peachy. The North American White Man: not so much. Because we had only one thing to depend on: everything we stole from the Teton Sioux, the Yanktonai, and the Plains Assiniboin. And now the Teton Sioux, the Yanktonai, and the Plains Assiniboin have taken it back.

Edward Curtis assumed The North American Indian did not know they were standing at the end of their history. He assumed that he needed to preserve the final, tragic, fleeting moments of their existence. To collect photographic samples of them. He needed to fix them in the permanent historical record like whoever had put the menagerie on Pontactico together had pickled, stuffed, and preserved the Hannibal Colossus, Roloff the Stuffed Russian Lobster Boy, the passenger pigeon, and the dead, naked, pickled, Pawhtnatawahta woman. But Edward Curtis was only half right: The North American Indian did not know they were standing at the end of their history because they weren't standing at the end of their history. Their history, and the history of the Kwakiutl, and the Teton Sioux, the Yanktonai, and the Plains Assiniboin would go on long after The White Man of North America had vanished. Because "Trees", and buffalo, and the passenger pigeon. And because "Ghost Dance".

I assumed America (or what was left of it, at least) would appreciate all my brutal, unflinching truth with the optimism of someone who has never had the searchlight of brutal, unflinching truth turned on themselves. But the brutal, unflinching truth was that I had already been exposed to the brutal, unflinching truth, I just didn't know it at the time: in volume 13 of "The North American Indian": the Paiute, and the Paiute prophet

Wovoka. And the Ghost Dance. Which Wovoka had been told would drive The North American White Man off the Paiute land, and off the Kwakiutl land, and off the Teton Sioux land, and the Yanktonai and the Plains Assiniboin land. While Uwe was busy building his fortune, and Pontactico, and the menagerie on Pontactico, the Kwakiutl, Teton Sioux, Yanktonai and Plains Assiniboin were busy trying to avoid genocide (small pox, repeating rifles, land theft, wiping out the buffalo and the passenger pigeon). The future had been revealed to Wovoka in a vision, and while the details were a little fuzzy (Wovoka, for example, did not foresee the Great Funk Crash) in the end he was proven correct. Wovoka got the time frame wrong. It never happened in his lifetime. And he got the "how" wrong. Wovoka thought his vision had told him the resurrected Paiute dead would drive out The White Man of North America. The resurrected Paiute dead did not drive out The White Man of North America. Trees did.

The library on Pontactico, in addition to having numerous fuckable 150-year-old sofa cushions, also contained an extensive library. Granted it was a library that seemed to have come to a sudden, screeching halt well before the Woodrow Wilson administration. It was particularly strong in the First Nations/ Indigenous Peoples departments, with a minor in medical disasters and abominations. What the connection was I have no idea. Just as I have no clear conception of exactly who or what or why Pontactico was built. Included in the library was a complete set of Jackson's beloved Edward S. Curtis opus "The North American Indian", which was an exhaustive photographic record of the Indigenous People of North America in 20 handsome, leather-bound, gilt-edged volumes. For reasons I cannot, or choose not to fathom, I gravitated instead towards the exhaustive collection of medical texts. Or perhaps "medical" might be a tad flattering. Mostly they contained terrifying black and white photographs of almost every medical malady, misfortune, mishap and breakdown that could befall a human being, made twenty to forty percent more terrifying by the knowledge that the pictures were taken at a time when the options available for treatment of all the maladies, misfortunes, mishaps and breakdowns was basically "wait and see if it clears up on its own" or simply "chop it off".

The contents of the library on Pontactico forced a binary choice on me and Jackson: aboriginal, or medical; Kwakiutl, Teton Sioux, Yanktonai and Plains Assiniboin, or tumors, goiters, deformities, the electrodactyl, the hydroencephalytic, and rickets. A choice between an epic chronicle of some of the most advanced and complete and noble and beautiful cultures the world has ever known, and a never ending catastrophe of medical disasters. I chose the never ending catastrophe of medical disasters. Not that I didn't enjoy the pictures of the Kwakiutl, Teton Sioux, Yanktonai and Plains Assiniboin. I found them haunting and inspiring. They made me jealous that I was not Kwakiutl, Teton Sioux, Yanktonai or Plains Assiniboin. But the medical disasters were compelling to me. I could not stop looking at them even as they shocked and repelled me. And I think they occupied the same space the Kwakiutl, Teton Sioux, Yanktonai and Plains Assiniboin occupied for Jackson: another entire world populated by another entire people. Only instead of other-worldly war paint and ceremonial garb, my community had tumors, goiters, deformities, were electrodactyl, hydroencephalytic and warped by rickets. In retrospect, I think we both found our own tribes. But what we did not find, and which seems odd to me as I write this, was any record of the Pawhtnatawahta in any of the 20 volumes of Edward Curtis's "The North American Indian".

No record of the Pawhtnatawahta exists in the library on Pontactico. But absence of evidence and evidence of absence are two separate things: it all gives me the creepy feeling this memoir is my own version of "The North American Indian". Except it should be called "The Van Kruups of Pontactico" and does not have any sepia pictures of me, or Uncle Roo, or my big brother Jackson staring out from its pages in noble, unbroken spirit despite the all-you-can-enjoy shit buffet helpfully provided by The North American White Man. And like The North American Indian, our numbers too were decimated. Not by small pox, repeating rifles, land theft, exterminating the passenger pigeon and the buffalo but by jetpack mishap, stepping down the elevator shaft of The Empire State Building and running away to live among, and study, and get eaten by, the Kwakiutl. There are no pictures of us unvanquished in spirit, or dressed in the traditional attire of my people. Unless you consider a picture of me dressed as Henry VIII the traditional attire of my people. And in this picture I am not staring, noble and unbroken into the photographer's lens. I am jerking off resolutely to the dead, naked, pickled Pawhtnatawahta woman in the menagerie. While Gay Sasquatch watches.

The truth was, watching Jackson fuck the 150-year-old sofa cushion put the fear of God in me. Because there was something in the menagerie that bore more than a passing resemblance to the 150-year-old sofa cushion: Roloff, the Stuffed Russian Lobster Boy. And I think this is where the nature/nurture argument comes into effect. Because I wasn't aware of having any feelings towards Roloff, the Stuffed Russian Lobster Boy. But then again I wasn't aware of having feeling for the dead, naked, pickled Pawhtnatawahta woman before I saw the dead, naked, pickled Pawhtnatawahta woman and started jerking off to the dead, naked, pickled Pawhtnatawahta woman. But I knew me and Jackson shared a sizable portion of our DNA. And it didn't seem an enormous leap, thematically speaking, from a 150-year-old sofa cushion to Roloff the Stuffed Russian Lobster Boy. So I felt I needed to know for sure if I felt anything toward Roloff. I wanted to find out as soon as possible. To just get it over with. So I forced myself to jerk off remorselessly while looking at Roloff the Stuffed Russian Lobster Boy, his football shaped head with dead, bulging crab eyes, and my relief was visceral when I felt no jolt of interest. Then, just to be safe, believing that, based on what finding Jackson fucking the 150-year-old sofa cushion in the library had done to our relationship, I took Roloff the Stuffed Russian Lobster Boy out of the menagerie to the front lawn, doused him with kerosene and burnt him to ashes. Then I burnt the ashes.

Jackson was my big brother and my idol and he cracked the cipher of sticking your dick in things. Which, while it may not sound like a major accomplishment, I think was pretty impressive considering we were raised in the middle of 10,000 acres of forest in total isolation. And then to make the quantum leap to sticking your dick in human females, I felt, and feel to this day, was a feat of Copernican, of Newtonian accomplishment. A discovery that changed the way we lived every day. The way we look at and interpret the world around us. Or a testament to simple probability. Because, to be honest, I don't know for certain what Jackson had or had not stuck his dick in before the 150-year-old cushion (absence of evidence/evidence of absence). The sort of "million monkeys on a million typewriters" scenario that I believe is (after Funk) the greatest animating force in the universe. For all I know, the 150-year-old sofa cushion might have been the *first* thing Jackson stuck his dick in. And even I'm assuming that was on purpose. I cannot rule out the possibility that he tripped, fell, and his dick landed in the 150-year-old sofa cushion. But unlike me and the dead, naked, pickled, Pawhtna-tawahta woman, Jackson was destined for greater things (or, at the very least different things). Or, at least, human things. Human things to fuck. Because it wouldn't be long before Jackson would trip, fall, and stick his dick in Frenchmans Bend, the small town at the base of the road that leads up to Pontactico.

Which was the beginning of the end for me and our life together on Pontactico. Which fills me with so many mixed feelings. In that I'm glad Jackson found his true calling. Or at least found the thing he wanted to stick his dick in: human females.

But since there were no living human females on Pontactico, sticking his dick in live, human females meant leaving Pontactico. And leaving me. And leaving me meant I would have no one to animate my days with hate and love, envy, confusion, admiration, contempt and endless quests for approval and disdain for his approval in the unlikely event I actually got it. All the contradictions that come with being a younger brother. In the end, I'm sure of only one thing: I'm grateful that for his first sexual experience he didn't trip, fall, and stick his dick in Roloff the Stuffed Russian Lobster Boy.

Then again, I do have to face the reality that if Jackson did trip, fall, and stick his dick in Roloff the Stuffed Russian Lobster Boy, he might've liked it. Sticking his dick in Roloff the Stuffed Russian Lobster Boy might've been his jam. I don't think anyone should have to defend their sexual orientation, preferences or peccadillos to anyone. I don't think anyone was hurt or injured by me jerking off to the dead, naked, pickled Pawhtnatawahta woman. I know that technically my predilection could be considered necrophilia (or, as I would prefer "thanatophilia"), but I didn't *actively* involve the dead. I committed no physical indignity to the dead. I inflicted no mental trauma on the dead, naked, pickled Pawhtnatawahta woman. Mainly because she was already dead, naked, and pickled. Unlike the creators of the menagerie, I had no hand in her preparation. It's like a tree falling in the forest: if a midget (or if you prefer, "little person") jerks off to a dead, naked, pickled Pawhtnatawahta woman and there's no one around to see it, does it really count? I feel like if brutal, unflinching truth belonged anywhere in this book it is probably here. Note: I have declared a temporary moratorium on brutal, unflinching truth.

Instead, I will throw myself on the mercy of the court: being raised in the middle of 10,000 acres, alone, how was I to know that jerking off to a dead, naked, pickled Pawhtnatawahta woman was wrong or in any way even objectionable? How was I supposed to know fucking a 150-year-old sofa cushion was in any way not part of every red blooded American male's sex life? For all I knew, the sum total of everyone's sex life outside Pontactico might've consisted *exclusively* of fucking a 150-year-old sofa cushion and jerking off to a dead, naked, pickled Pawhtnatawahta woman. If anyone should've been mortified by finding Jackson fucking a 150-year-old sofa cushion it should've been me. Because as far as I knew, as far as my limited personal experience ran, jerking off to a dead, naked, pickled Pawhtnatawahta woman was normal, and fucking a 150-year-old sofa cushion in the library on Pontactico was sick and worthy of derision. For all I know now, after all I've seen of sexuality outside Pontactico (Gay Sasquatch and his orangutan lover Professor University, the homicidal sodomites of Ohio gang-raping people to death) I think both fucking a 150-year-old sofa cushion and jerking off to a dead, naked, pickled Pawhtnatawahta woman seem pretty soft focus by comparison. All I'm saying is there are worse crimes in the world than fucking a 150-year-old sofa cushion and jerking off to a dead, naked, pickled Pawhtnatawahta woman. And yes, I include fucking Roloff, the Stuffed Russian Lobster Boy in this category. Word of honor: I have never fucked Roloff, the Stuffed Russian Lobster Boy. Word of honor: I do not want to fuck Roloff, the Stuffed Russian Lobster Boy. Or a 150-year-old sofa cushion. My policy on dead, naked, pickled Pawhtnatawahta women is an open book.

All this is not to say I didn't have some false starts, some successive approximations, before I discovered my true calling. Consider, if you will, the medical texts in the library, on Pontactico: my first experience with the human body. My first experience with the naked human body. My first experience with the malformed, goitered, herniated, pinheaded, smallpox riven naked human body. That's how I knew Roloff the Stuffed Russian Boy was "electrodactyl": I had seen pictures of a naked electrodactyl in the medical texts in the library on Pontactico. But I did not end up jerking off to pictures of malformed, goitered, herniated, pinheaded, smallpox riven naked human bodies. I know this is a strange claim to fame, a strange hook to hang my hat on, but it is the brutal, unflinching truth nonetheless (game on).

The medical textbooks were all state of the art. As long as the state of that art was before almost every major development in modern medicine save germ theory. So I'm not exactly sure what the value of diagnosing all those horrifying conditions even was. It's not like they could do anything for about eighty percent of even the most basic medical conditions. So the only purpose would seem to be to inform the unlucky patient exactly what horrifying condition they had, how that horrifying condition was going to progress, and then how that horrifying condition would kill them, usually in a horrifying, drawn out, and excruciating process. Which means there was really no purpose beyond the encyclopedically prurient. It was as if, overcharged with the possibilities of the new medium of mass-photography someone (or, most likely, a bunch of someones) had decided to document every possible medical nightmare and misfortune simply for the fuck of it. That the entire collection of photographs was assembled either by one very determined man (presumably in a top hat and stroking a waxed mustache, armed with a tripod camera) gaining access by God knows how to God knows what hospitals, asylums and poor houses and somehow convincing the people who ran those hospitals, asylums and poor houses to let him take pictures of random people who were the victims of random medical nightmares. How exactly do you talk your way into that scenario? The other (possibly more terrifying option?): a national cabal of low level orderlies offering access to low level weirdos with cameras hoping to supplement their presumably low income positions in various state run hospitals, asylums and poor houses in which they were employed and entrusted with the safety and dignity of their charges. Were the photos bought and sold, traded as part of some secret underground cabal? And yet some shred of decency (and here I use the word loosely) seemed to remain (as much human decency you could attribute to someone after they had stripped a helpless human being with startling deformities naked with (best case scenario) limited consent) and taken their picture for mass distribution.

The pictures of the people had their eyes inked out with a horizontal black banner, presumably to conceal their identities. Or, now that I think about it, more likely to conceal the identity of their chronicler: since the chain of evidence from someone with a rare medical condition that just happened to get stripped naked, get their picture taken, and then whoever took that picture circulating it to a circle of fellow aficionados would be a short one. But my point is a simple one: why did I not become someone with a predilection for the naked, deformed and disfigured? Why did I not spend my adult life skulking in alleyways waiting to make connections to complete my personal photographic collection with someone with a case of childhood rickets, naked pinheads, or elephantiasis of the balls? Why, with the fortune at my disposal, was I not simply traveling the world (in an atomic powered 707 perhaps?), arriving at service entrances of every hospital and asylum in the world in the small hours of the morning with a complete camera crew? And if that was the case, then considering the resources at my command, peopling all of Pontactico with a personal collection of those poor souls. Perhaps a movie studio? Carefully mapped out and scripted and staged epics? Othello as performed by an entire cast of pinheads? Long Day's Journey Into Night made just that much more poignant by an ensemble cast all with elephantiasis of the balls? The imagination runs riot. But I did not.

The deformities, the by-products of lack of micro-nutrients, the manifestations of genetic free form jazz did not take. Roloff did not take. Only the dead, naked, pickled Pawhtnatawahta woman took. I saw Roloff first, propped against one of the wooden cases containing all the samples of birds, butterflies, plants and minerals in the menagerie, as if casually placed there temporarily and then forgotten about. Granted, Roloff was not naked, so I am forced to reduce his over/under for the odds of his permanently warping my sex life into one of the sub-genres that may or may not have made my life easier. Granted Roloff did have portability in his favor, something the dead, naked, pickled Pawhtnatawahta woman did not. Granted if Roloff had turned my crank I might've been saved a lifetime of sexual fumbling, confusion, frustration and longing for something I wanted but could not name, something I thirsted for. Like a mineral my body craved but of which I was not consciously aware. A sort of sexual scurvy, if you will. I might've spent my entire life wondering what everybody thought was so great about sex. What all the fuss was about. Not understanding that all the sex I had experienced just wasn't the sex I was wired for: sex with a dead, naked, stuffed-like-a-sofa-cushion Russian electrodactyl.

Chapter 5

This is a story about America and jerking off. And fratricide: I killed my older brother Jackson. I did not smite (smote?) him with the jawbone of an ass. We were not Cain and Abel. I embarrassed him to death. By stumbling on him fucking a 150-year-old sofa cushion in the library on Pontactico. By getting caught watching him fuck a girl in Frenchmans Bend, dressed as Napoleon (me, not Jackson). By Jackson catching me jerking off for the Kennedys dressed as Kaiser Wilhelm II complete with pickelhaube (me, not Jackson). But most of all by the photograph of me, taken from the orbiting Empire State Building, jerking off to the dead, naked, pickled Pawhtnatawahta woman in the menagerie on Pontactico. Dressed as Henry VIII. While Gay Sasquatch watched.

Jackson was so embarrassed by everyone knowing that he had a brother who jerked off to a dead, naked, pickled Pawhtnatawahta woman while dressed as Henry VIII while Gay Sasquatch watched that he attempted to escape everyone knowing that he had a brother who jerked off to a dead, naked, pickled Pawhtnatawahta woman while dressed as Henry VIII while Gay Sasquatch watched by running away to live among, and study, and get eaten by the Kwakiutl. This was not my intent. I did not want to kill Jackson. I just wanted his respect. Or something in the same zip code as respect. I would've accepted "confused indifference". I held out hope that confused indifference might grow to "puzzled concern". When you are a younger brother, you take what you can get.

$ $ $

The photograph of me, jerking off to the dead, naked, pickled Pawhtnatawahta woman while dressed as Henry VIII while Gay Sasquatch watched should've been a political scandal. Presidents have been impeached for less. I'm not sure what section of the constitution "jerking off to a dead, naked, pickled Pawhtnatawahta woman, dressed as Henry VIII while Gay Sasquatch watched" would contravene, but I think there at least should have been some blowback. There was no blowback. That's how bad things had gotten when I became President. The other option: no one cared because I was a midget (or, if you prefer, "little person"). Because people seemed to expect a midget (or, if you prefer, "little person") to just do shit like that. Or at the very least, not to be judged by the same standards as a regular sized person caught jerking off to a dead, naked, pickled Pawhtnatawahta woman, while dressed as Henry VIII, while Gay Sasquatch watched. It seemed to fall under a sort of "Gentlemen's Agreement" between regular sized people and little people. Which seemed related to the unspoken contract between regular people and people with lobster claws where their hands should be. Or Pawhtnatawahta women. But not regular sized people having sex with other regular sized people while their midget younger brother watched dressed as Napoleon. So Jackson got labeled a Sex Weirdo, while my sex life simply became a low-brow punchline for the same tabloids that had made fun of Jimmy, the super fat guy from Cleveland who was so huge he couldn't even make it out of his own house.

$ $ $

I never found out who took that picture of me jerking off to the dead, naked, pickled Pawhtnatawahta woman while dressed as Henry VIII while Gay Sasquatch watched. Technically, therefore, I cannot say for one hundred percent sure that it was taken from the orbiting Empire State Building. It could've been taken from the orbiting Statue of Liberty. Or even the Houston Astrodome on the moon where that asshole who wouldn't leave Jimmy, the super fat guy from Cleveland alone had hit the World

Series winning home run. I thought that maybe when I became President I would find out who took the picture. There would be Congressional Committees. There would be Grand Jury Subpoenas. There *were* Congressional Committees. There *were* Grand Jury Subpoenas. But we never found out who took the picture.

Not finding out who took the picture of me jerking off to the dead, naked, pickled Pawhtnatawahta woman while dressed as Henry VIII while Gay Sasquatch watched was just one in a long list of things I would not find out when I became President. Like where the Trees came from. Or where the pilots of the UFOs I was shown at Roswell came from. Technically, shaking hands with Gay Sasquatch beneath a full moon under the rotunda of the Jefferson Memorial was not a secret: Gay Sasquatch had already saved my life on Pontactico. I did not know Gay Sasquatch was gay. It was none of my business. I only found out later, when Gay Sasquatch showed up to be sworn in as my Secretary of the Interior with his partner, Professor University, the orangutan who had previously been employed jerking off for peanuts, cotton candy, and hot dogs for the all-primate Houston Astros (back when the Houston Astrodome was still safely back on earth). So when I told everyone in America in my first State of the Union Address that Gay Sasquatch saved my life, people started putting that on T-shirts too: "GAY SASQUATCH SAVED MY LIFE". And young people wore the T-shirt, not to show they were sick and tired of everything like when they wore the "TOO FAT TO GO TO THE MOON" T-shirt, but to show they were maybe a little bit hopeful about the world and how just because you were gay or eight feet tall and covered all over in hair or got off by jerking off to a dead, naked, pickled Pawhtnatawahta woman while dressed as Henry VIII while Gay Sasquatch watched, you could still be accepted in society and not made to feel bad about who or what you are.

$ $ $

By the time I became President everybody had seen the picture of me jerking off to the dead, naked, pickled Pawhtnatawahta woman, while dressed as Henry VIII while Gay Sasquatch watched, but no one seemed to care. But they did care when they found out about Jackson fucking someone while his midget (or, if you prefer "little person") younger brother watched, dressed as Napoleon. Which upset me for a couple reasons. Mostly I was offended by the lack of outrage and indignation at finding out the most powerful man in the world got his rocks off by jerking off to a dead, naked, pickled Pawhtnatawahta woman while dressed as Henry VIII while Gay Sasquatch watched. But they were deeply offended that Jackson could only get off by having sex while I watched dressed as Napoleon. Because I was the common denominator in both sex-degenerate scenarios: a midget dressed in period costume (and here I'll leave out the "or, if you prefer, "little person"" part, because the newspapers never called me a little person. They called me a midget). They said that the only way Jackson could get off was by having sex with women while his midget younger brother watched dressed as Napoleon (they didn't know about the other period costumes: Kaiser Wilhelm II complete with pickelhaub, Julius Caesar, Henry VIII and Abraham Lincoln).

No one ever called me a midget to my face. They always called me a little person. But I knew they were thinking "midget". And regardless, I knew that whatever word they used, like calling Roloff, the stuffed Russian Lobster Boy "Roloff the Electrodactyl", they could still stuff Roloff like a sofa cushion and sell him off for someone's menagerie. Just like regardless if they called me a midget or a little person, they were free to think of me automatically as a sex-degenerate who could only get off by jerking off to a dead, naked, pickled Pawhtnatawahta woman while dressed as Henry VIII while Gay Sasquatch watched. And I think it's entirely beside the point that jerking off to a dead, naked, pickled Pawhtnatawahta woman while dressed as Henry

VIII while Gay Sasquatch watched *was* the only way I could get my rocks off. Like when they assumed Jackson's only source of gratification was fucking women while I watched dressed as Napoleon, I wanted them to be outraged at me and disgusted by me having as my only sex outlet jerking off to a dead, naked, pickled Pawhtnatawahta woman while dressed as Henry VIII while Gay Sasquatch watched. Instead, they just assumed that because I was a midget, it must come as no particular surprise that I was also a sex weirdo. Granted, I *was* a sex weirdo, but that's neither here nor there. They got it just plain wrong: I did not know I was being watched by Gay Sasquatch at the time. So I would've been, if not overjoyed, then at least resigned to them judging me for jerking off to a dead, naked, pickled Pawhtnatawahta woman. Just not for judging me for jerking off to a dead, naked, pickled Pawhtnatawahta woman while Gay Sasquatch watched. But because I was a midget, no one was really required to care. It didn't piss me off that people knew I could only get off by jerking off to a dead, naked, pickled Pawhtnatawahta woman while dressed as Henry VIII while Gay Sasquatch watched. It pissed me off that people didn't seem surprised or bothered by it. It pissed me off because the implication seemed to be that, as a midget, I was obviously a freak, and therefore I must have freaky midget sex habits. Granted I *did* have freaky midget sex habits, but again, I must insist this is a red herring.

$ $ $

It's not like me jerking off to a dead, naked, pickled Pawhtnatawahta woman while dressed as Henry VIII while Gay Sasquatch watched was a secret. That is, if anybody had asked me, I would've told them. I think. Except for the part about being watched by Gay Sasquatch. Which I did not know about at the time. It was a secret even from me. I found out at the same time as everybody else: when that picture of me jerking off to a dead, naked, pickled Pawhtnatawahta woman while dressed as Henry VIII while Gay Sasquatch watched showed up in the tabloids.

Like most Americans, I thought the President must have access to President level secrets. And like most Americans I assumed these secrets must trend toward the conspiratorial, the science fiction, the underpants soiling. Like finding out Time Traveling Lizard People really run the planet. Or the Rothschilds. Or Time Traveling Lizard Rothschilds. But the only underpants soiling factoid about who secretly ran the world was that no one was secretly running the world. There was no cabal of super rich elite/Time Traveling Lizard Rothschilds planning war and engineering famine and a nickel hike in the price of gasoline over the Labor Day weekend. And believe me, I really wish they did tell me Time Traveling Lizard Rothschilds ran the world. At least that way, as a puppet potentate, I would be off the hook for any real responsibility for which I might have to answer to the American people, and eventually the judgment of history. Because I was about as qualified to run the world as a three-legged cocker spaniel.

The biggest underpants soiling secret I found out as President was that there were no underpants soiling secrets waiting for me when I became President. I read in the FDR biography in the library of the Cultural Education Center in Albany that Truman (FDR's Vice President) only found out about the Manhattan Project and the completion of the atomic bomb after FDR died. As Commander in Chief of our nation's armed forces, I would've been privy to any equivalent, underpants soiling information when I became President. The other option being that they did not trust me with any of their underpants soiling secrets. They would have good reason: I did not inspire confidence in them. I could not even learn the different Defense Readiness Conditions (or "DEFCON" levels). I don't think it was unrealistic of the Joint Chiefs of Staff to expect the President to know the different DEFCON levels. I could not learn the different DEFCON levels.

$ $ $

The DEFCON scale, indicating the state of readiness our nation's armed forces were supposed to assume, was composed of colors, and it was composed of numbers, and it was composed of terms. The numbers ran from 1 to 4 (I think), but I could not remember if 4 was "bend over and kiss your ass goodbye" or 1 was. Same with the colors. One of the colors was blue. But I could not remember whether blue meant "all clear" or "bend over and kiss your ass goodbye". And then there were the terms to go along with each DEFCON level. The only one of which I can remember was the underpants soiling "cocked pistol". But like I said, whether "cocked pistol" was 4, 1, blue or fucking paisley, I do not remember. And I could not remember when I was President. Which did not seem to particularly bother my Chiefs of Staff. Which puzzled me at the time, as the information seemed important. Knowing whether America is about to be incinerated into a giant piece of obsidian glass in a nanosecond seems like something the President should know. But it turns out I didn't have to know. Because Gay Sasquatch knew (sleep tight, America).

$ $ $

I could not remember the DEFCON levels, and I could not remember the command structure of all the armed forces I was supposed to command in the event that America found itself at the underpants soiling "cocked pistol" state of potential nuclear war. I know all my Chiefs of Staff were Generals or Admirals, but that was about it. Then there was just everybody else (sorry "everybody else" in our nation's armed forces). Some of them had eagles, if I remember correctly. A lot had stripes. Some had bars. Some had more bars than others. The more bars the better. I think. Then there was the Neapolitan ice cream selection of campaign ribbons. Again: none of this seemed to bother my Chiefs of Staff. Again: because I did not need to know. Because Gay Sasquatch knew.

$ $ $

I did not know that Gay Sasquatch knew all the things I was supposed to know as President. I did not know Gay Sasquatch knew many things I was *not* supposed to know. And most importantly, all the time I was President, I did not know Gay Sasquatch had a higher security clearance than me. Higher than the President. Which meant he had to be careful what he said around me (and also what he said around Professor University, his orangutan life-partner for that matter. Which at times drove a tremendous wedge between them believe you me) because he might let slip something about the Gay Sasquatch Level Secrets he knew.

I did not know Gay Sasquatch's security clearance level. That's how high it was: so high I wasn't even allowed to know what it was. But even if I did know, if I had been told, I'm pretty confident I would not have been able to remember it. Or even if I had, like the different DEFCON levels and like the military command structure, where it fit in the order of the overall security levels. I was told the security levels. And then I promptly forgot the security levels. I knew Top Secret was above "Secret", but there was also "Ultra Top Secret" (I think) and "Burn After Reading" (that one I remember because it felt so cool burning the message after reading the message that was so secret you literally had to burn it after reading it). But I can't remember if "Burn After Reading" came before, after, or was at the same level as "Ultra Top Secret" (or if "Ultra Top Secret" even exists or I simply made it up). And why Gay Sasquatch had a higher security clearance than me, as President, was never revealed to me. Or what his actual security level was. So I can only refer to it as "Gay Sasquatch Level Secret".

$ $ $

When I was sworn in as President I was not told Time Traveling Lizard Rothschilds ran the world. I know what you're thinking: as one of America's super rich elite, as one of those who would directly benefit from serious face time with our Time Traveling Lizard Rothschild Overlords, I would never tell you that we are (were?) ruled over by Time Traveling Lizard Rothschilds. But since now, in this AT world, in this "catamites as the new normal" world, I don't think it would be difficult to convince you no one is in charge. What have I got to lose? And I'm not saying Time Traveling Lizard Rothschilds *don't* run the world. I'm just saying that, as President, I was never shown any evidence that Time Traveling Lizard Rothschilds ran the world. And that seems like information a President should have access to. As President I was not given this information. Which leads me to one possible conclusion: Time Traveling Lizard People do not run the world, Gay Sasquatch does. And I never had the stones to ask him directly if he ran the world, presumably with a cabal of other Sasquatches (and here I must assume, for the sake of argument, that Sasquatches run the full spectrum of LGBTQ/ Two Spirit Continuum of Sasquatch sexuality). And even if I had asked him I'm pretty sure he wouldn't have told me, because "Gay Sasquatch Level Secrets" (or, to be entirely factual, "LGBTQ/Two Spirit Continuum Sasquatch Secrets").

$ $ $

When I became President, when I tried to tell the American people that there was no Super Rich Elite running America, they assumed I said this because I was one of the Super Rich Elites that ran America. I was, after all, a member of one of America's richest families. But that was before the Great Funk Crash cleaned us out and left me with the sum of our family fortune totaling

$367.32 in a brown paper lunch bag. And I never got a chance to tell America that the Van Kruup family had been cleaned out by the Great Funk Crash, because "Trees". And I did not have the nerve, after their response to seeing Itsy-Bitsy FDR piss a perfect one ounce shot of bourbon, to tell them that Gay Sasquatch really ran America. Or at the very least was higher up in the pecking order of American power than me. So high he couldn't even tell me how high or how he got there. So everyone simply assumed Father (being a card-carrying member of America's Super Rich Ruling Elite) had engineered the Great Funk Crash to make even more money. The fact that Trees ensured that, even if we had increased our already colossal fortune, we would have nothing to spend it on, did not seem to register. It was assumed that we had some sort of secret lair (we did: it was called "Greenbrier", but the only thing we could spend money on there was soda and pinball, and they were free), or that I had taken our fortune and travelled across space, or time, or something, to some distant galaxy, with our entire fortune converted into some sort of transgalactic fungible currency that I could spend on all sort of exotic, interstellar luxuries and sensual pleasures of a deeply degenerate nature (if you are reading this you know I did not travel across time or space, that getting to Albany was challenge enough).

Before the Great Funk Crash, I tried to calm the American people. I tried telling the brutal, unflinching truth to the American people. I told them about Gay Sasquatch. I told them about Greenbrier. I told them about the UFOs at Roswell. I promised that, no matter what, I would trust the American people. I would have faith in the intelligence and good judgment of the American people. That if we had discovered time travel, or who had really killed JFK, or that the Bermuda Triangle really existed, or that Hitler was alive and well and living in Indianapolis, I would trust them to know this information, this secret knowledge, and trust them not to freak the fuck out about it. And I believed this.

More or less. Give or take. Mainly because I had zero experience dealing with the American people. Or people in general. So I did not know that under no circumstances should they be trusted with this secret knowledge. That the last thing the American people wanted from their President was the brutal, unflinching truth. I discovered that, as a member of the Super Rich Ruling Elite, there were sound reasons for keeping the truth from the American people. Mainly the fact that if the American people knew the truth, they would flip the fuck out. Which is why I did not tell them who really killed JFK. Why I did not tell them that the Bermuda Triangle was real. And most of all I did not tell them Hitler was alive and well and living in Indianapolis. Because he was not alive and well and living in Indianapolis. Hitler was alive and well, and living on Pontactico.

$ $ $

When I first became President, before I found out the last thing the American people wanted was brutal, unflinching truth, I was determined to follow a policy of brutal, unflinching truth. I went before Congress and told them my secrets. I told them about Jackson fucking the 150-year-old sofa cushion. I told them about me jerking off to the dead, naked, pickled Pawhtnatawahta woman. I went before Congress, wearing a TOO FAT TO GO TO THE MOON T-shirt and told them Gay Sasquatch saved my life. When I said the part about Gay Sasquatch I leaned solemnly into the microphone, in front of the television cameras, moving my eye contact down the long table of Senators and Representatives. "Gay Sasquatch saved my life," I said. I hoped my tone would convey the gravity of the events I had witnessed, my sincere intent to only share the brutal, unflinching truth with the American people. I wanted "Gay Sasquatch saved my life" to be right up there with "we have nothing to fear but fear itself" and "ask not what your country can do for you, but what you can do for your country". But instead there was simply an un-comprehending silence, as if they were unsure if I was speaking literally, metaphorically, or attempting to indicate some sort of deeper truth by analogy. And in the moment before I moved on, before I told them Time Traveling Hitler killed their former President, Itsy-Bitsy Bourbon Pissing FDR jumped up on the table beside me, yelped out in his unmistakable mid-Atlantic accent "we have nothing to fear, but fear itself!", and promptly pissed a perfect one ounce shot of well-oaked Tennessee corn whiskey into my water glass. Then, in response to my brutally unflinching testimony before the Congressional committee, the Funk Market Crashed. That's how I learned the hard lesson that the American people were not ready for the brutal, unflinching truth. Which made me glad I did not tell them about Gay Time Traveling Hitler. And that Gay Time Traveling Hitler, like the FDR who had just pissed a one ounce shot of bourbon in front of the American people on live television, was itsy-bitsy.

$ $ $

That's how I found out Itsy-Bitsy Bourbon Pissing FDR was Itsy-Bitsy Bourbon Pissing FDR: on live television in front of Congress and the American people. It was a secret even from me. Not that I think Itsy-Bitsy Bourbon Pissing FDR was purposely keeping this information from me. It just never really came up. But everyone just assumed I was keeping this secret from them. Which was partially true. I wasn't technically keeping his existence from them, I just didn't know about the bourbon pissing part. Also, I didn't know what order to tell the American people all the secrets in. I did not know which one was my show stopper. In retrospect, Itsy-Bitsy Bourbon Pissing FDR pissing a perfect one ounce shot of delicious Tennessee-style corn whiskey was probably my show stopper. These days, of course, everyone knows that all you need to do to get Itsy-Bitsy Bourbon Pissing

FDR to piss a perfect one ounce shot of delicious Tennessee-style corn whiskey is to present him with a shot glass. Otherwise it seems to depend more or less on their individual affinity for individual glassware: sometimes a rock glass will produce this reflex. Other times a snifter, highball, or cosmopolitan cocktail glass may do the trick. In retrospect I think the American people would've been less traumatized if I had told them the Van Kruups were a family of Time Traveling Lizard People, that the Mafia killed JFK, and the moon landings were faked. We might have even gotten away with avoiding the Great Funk Crash. But Itsy-Bitsy Bourbon Pissing FDR had other ideas: he started with his show stopper.

$ $ $

"GAY SASQUATCH SAVED MY LIFE" did not stir the consciousness of the American people like "We have nothing to fear but fear itself". It didn't even make it on to a T-shirt, as far as I know. Because no one could figure out what the fuck I was talking about. And there wasn't a lot of time to explain because the American people seeing Itsy-Bitsy Bourbon Pissing FDR pissing a perfect one ounce shot of bourbon freaked them out so much the Funk Market crashed.

I don't know of any President who had to hit the ground running as fast as I did. And there was certainly no time to explain about Gay Time Traveling Hitler even if I had been able to bring it up in my address to Congress. How do I know Time Traveling Hitler was gay? That I can answer with empirical evidence: because I caught him jerking off to gay, stereoscopic 3d porn that last Thanksgiving in Tiny Town.

$ $ $

Facts about Tiny Town:

Fact No. 1: Tiny Town is tiny (self explanatory).

Fact No. 2: Tiny Town is not full of tiny people. At some point in the medium far away history of Pontactico, Tiny Town's population had been evacuated en masse, sometime in the era of "tooth powders" and "nerve tonics".

Fact No.3: the tiny inhabitants of Tiny Town had disproportionally large collections of pornography. Stereoscopic, 3d pornography.

Addendum to Fact No. 3: in all fairness to the tiny people of Tiny Town, I cannot state empirically that their pornography collections were disproportionally large. To state this as fact would require a survey of the size of the pornography collections of regular sized people. Fact: I did not conduct a survey of the pornography collections of regular sized people.

$ $ $

Stereoscopic 3d porn: the porn was printed on a sort of oversized postcard. The oversized postcard was placed in a viewer and focused. It was a very popular medium a long time ago. A time when people used things like tooth powders and nerve tonics. Almost every house in Tiny Town had collections of these oversized postcards. Most featured places and events that were either historic, or things no one but the extremely wealthy in those days could afford to travel to see in person: the Eiffel Tower, the Great Pyramids, and so on. And historic events: like Abraham Lincoln giving the Gettysburg Address following the Battle of Gettysburg. I know this because I found an oversized postcard of Abraham Lincoln giving the Gettysburg Address: complete with top hat, creepy half-beard, clawhammer top coat, one hand holding the paper on which was written the Gettysburg Address. The other hand proudly holding a fully engorged penis.

$ $ $

There was an oversized postcard of Abraham Lincoln with a proud, stereoscopic stiffy. There was an oversized postcard of Napoleon with a proud, stereoscopic 3d stiffy. There were over-sized postcards of Julius Caesar, Henry VIII, and Kaiser Wilhelm II complete with pickelhaube, all with proud stereoscopic 3d stiffies . To make a long story short, there was an entire collection of oversized postcards of our Great-Great-Great-Grand-father and family patriarch Uwe Van Kruup jerking off dressed as Abraham Lincoln, Julius Cesar, Henry VIII, Napoleon and Kaiser Wilhelm II complete with pickelhaube. And stereoscopic 3d stiffy.

At least I *think* it was our Great-Great-Great-Grandfather and family patriarch Uwe Van Kruup. I had no way of being one hundred percent certain. Granted, the odds of someone else fitting all of Uwe's costumes and being that extremely well hung had to be astronomically low, but it cannot be entirely ruled out. In the description on the oversized postcards of Abraham Lincoln, Napoleon, Kaiser Wilhelm II, Julius Caesar and Henry VIII jerking off, whoever was jerking off was identified not as "Uwe Van Kruup" but, with a touch I could not wholly decipher as an attempt at comedy, or merely factual as "The Commodore".

The only other clue was the fact that whoever was on the oversized postcards looked alarmingly like me. Or rather, me in early middle age. Or rather, almost the spitting image of Father. Which made me realize Father looked almost exactly like me. Only older. Which made Uwe an old me. Or maybe a time traveling me? A me from the future traveling back in time to deliver some ominous warning about some terrible fate about to befall us (Gay Time Traveling Hitler traveling to the future to kill me?). The only other clue was the address of the company that had made the oversized postcards. A company with the ersatz, tongue twisting name of "The East Philadelphia Novelty Watch Fob and Safe Striking Match Company". But the mailing address wasn't in Philadelphia. It was in Frenchmans Bend, just down the road from Pontactico.

$ $ $

I said that I found Gay Time Traveling Hitler jerking off to gay porn in Tiny Town. This is not entirely true. That is, the porn he was jacking off to wasn't specifically gay porn. He was jacking off to Uwe dressed as Abraham Lincoln, Napoleon, Kaiser Wilhelm II, Julius Caesar and Henry VIII. But that didn't make the porn itself necessarily "gay porn". And I couldn't say for absolute sure that Gay Hitler was a time traveller. At first I couldn't even necessarily say it was Hitler. But Hitler is kind of iconic. Hitler's brand is strong. And I assume he was gay, because almost every collection of stereoscopic 3d porn in Tiny Town had almost every conceivable type of porn. I know because I looked at them all (that is to say, every postcard in every collection of porn I found). This was not mere prurient interest on my part. When I found those porn stashes I realized I had been presented with a lucky accident, and an opportunity: to see if any of the porn would make me feel the way I did when I saw the dead, naked, pickled Pawhtnatawahta woman. Answer: none of the porn made me feel the way I did when I saw the dead, naked, pickled Pawhtnatawahta woman. Not the porn involving Abraham Lincoln, Napoleon, Kaiser Wilhelm II, Julius Caesar or Henry VIII. Not the porn involving live, naked women. None of the porn involving Uwe dressed as Abraham Lincoln, Napoleon, Kaiser Wilhelm II, Julius Caesar and Henry VIII and a pony. Or Abraham Lincoln, Napoleon, Kaiser Wilhelm II, Julius Caesar and

Henry VIII and a pony and a live, naked woman. Or Abraham Lincoln, Napoleon, Kaiser Wilhelm II, Julius Caesar and Henry VIII and a pony and midget (or if you prefer, "little person") woman. Or Abraham Lincoln, Napoleon, Kaiser Wilhelm II, Julius Caesar and Henry VIII and a pony and midget (or if you prefer, "little person") woman and an entire wedding cake. And so on. The collections were nothing if not encyclopedic. So, bit by bit, I began to make my way resolutely through all of it. The only one that worked: the oversized postcard of the dead, naked, pickled, Pawhtnatawahta woman.

$ $ $

I discovered the porn in Tiny Town in the months leading up to that final Thanksgiving on Pontactico because I was scouting out Tiny Town. Because I wanted to know why Father and my Uncle Roo and Uncle Dash and Jackson went there every Thanksgiving. Finding the porn did not clear things up any. Or at least they did not clear them up in any way I wanted them to be cleared up. Because the only reason I could figure out why they were all going to Tiny Town was to look at the porn in Tiny Town. Going *together* to look at the porn in Tiny Town. The porn composed of every possible result of the human sexual algorithm that had led me to do things like jerk off to a dead, naked, pickled Pawhtnatawahta woman and for Jackson to fuck a 150-year-old sofa cushion. And jerking off on a cracker.

$ $ $

I did not know much about my relatives' lives outside Pontactico, but I knew one thing: Uncle Dash used to jack off on a cracker. I knew this because Uncle Dash told Jackson. And then Jackson told me.

$ $ $

Father could make his brothers show up on Pontactico because he controlled The Van Kruup Family Trust. Father could make Uncle Dash go to Outer Space University because he controlled The Van Kruup Family Trust. Father did not make Uncle Dash jerk off on a cracker at Outer Space University. Uncle Dash did that on his own initiative.

$ $ $

Outer Space University was not called "Outer Space University". It was called "The Center for Advanced Interstellar Logistics and Propulsion". But once young people heard about it, and that Father owned it, and that it was basically bullshit, they started calling it Outer Space University. Then they put "OUTER SPACE UNIVERSITY" on T-shirts, mainly to show how they thought everything older people did was bullshit (like starting a bullshit college with the bullshit name of "The Center for Advanced Interstellar Logistics and Propulsion" that was concerned primarily with bullshit).

Father had started Outer Space University as a tax dodge as part of his plan to put all our national monuments in space. Then he made Uncle Dash go there to make it seem legit. Then he made Uncle Dash play on the Outer Space University Football Team. The Outer Space University Football Team wore jet packs, because "Outer Space University". When the Outer Space University Football Team (GO ROCKETS!) were not playing football (while wearing jet packs) they were jerking off on a cracker. That was how the Outer Space University Football Team settled all disputes: they stood in a circle around a cracker jerking off on a cracker. The last person to jerk off on the cracker had to eat the cracker.

$ $ $

"EAT THE CRACKER", by the way did find a brief vogue with young people, who put it on T-shirts to express the way they felt about the world, and how it was all going straight to shit, and how the only thing we could figure out to do was put the Statue of Liberty and Empire State Building into orbit. I even wore an EAT THE CRACKER T-shirt during my first appearance as President, on national television, shortly after I flew to the White House, shortly after I jerked off for the Kennedys, after Gay Time Traveling Hitler killed Father. I wore it to try to temper the expectations of the American people. To be brutally and unflinchingly honest about what the American people could expect from my new administration. To be brutally and unflinchingly truthful about the direction America was headed. Not exactly "It's morning in America", but I think fundamentally more honest.

$ $ $

Father wanted Jackson to go to Outer Space University. Jackson did not want to go to Outer Space University. Especially after Uncle Dash told him what the football team did for conflict resolution. I did not want Jackson to go to Outer Space University. And not just because EAT THE CRACKER. I didn't want to be left alone on Pontactico. Because Jackson was the sum total of what, to me constituted a family. Father, Uncle Roo, and Uncle Dash were technically family. But I only saw them once a year, on Thanksgiving. The other 364 days of the year it was just me and Jackson and my Irish wolf hounds Romulus and Remus. And Gay Sasquatch.

Jackson lived alone with me. But I think it's fair to say Jackson lived even more alone than me. Jackson had three interests in life: sports, fucking, and sport fucking. And the Kwakiutl. I was of no help in any of these undertakings. I had the athletic

ability of a cinder block. Strike that: a cinder block had more athletic ability than me. The only place Jackson could indulge his
interests was Frenchmans Bend, the town at the bottom of the
road that ran to Pontactico. Which is where I saw him pursuing
his interests with an increasing feverishness in the years leading
up to that last Thanksgiving. And Jackson really managed to put
up some impressive numbers. Because Jackson, like his uncles,
and unlike me and Father, was tall and handsome and athletic
and fuckable. His fuckability rating was high. I would hazard a
guess at top ten percentile. At least until that day I followed him
to Frenchmans Bend and got caught watching him fuck that girl
dressed as Napoleon (me, not the girl). I believe I can state that
few things kill your chances of getting laid like the widespread
knowledge that you enjoy fucking while your midget (or, if you
prefer, "little person") younger brother watches you dressed as
Napoleon. Possible exceptions: the widespread knowledge that
you enjoy fucking while your midget (or, if you prefer, "little
person") younger brother watches you dressed as Kaiser Wilhelm II, Julius Caesar, Henry VIII, or Abraham Lincoln.

$ $ $

I never thought to question why Father and my uncles chose to
abandon me on Pontactico for 364 days a year, and then to appear for a one night only engagement on Thanksgiving. I figured
"Thanksgiving" was reason enough. We were a family. Just like
the Kennedys and the Rockefellers were a family. The Kennedys got together for their holidays at Hyannis Port (I assumed).
The Rockefellers got together for their holidays on the orbiting
Empire State Building (after Father put the Empire State Building in space, of course). Normal American families got together
for normal American holidays: Christmas, Easter, Fourth of July,
and that most normal of all holidays: Thanksgiving. The math
just added up. But why I calculated that remainder from the long

division of a family composed of a midget (or, if you prefer, "little person"), a sex addict, a manic depressive, and a midget (or, if you prefer, "little person") who jacked off to a dead, naked, pickled Pawhtnatawahta woman, I cannot say. And outside the immediate family there wasn't exactly a ton of role models on our completely isolated 10,000 acres. Unless you consider Gay Sasquatch and an Itsy-Bitsy Bourbon Pissing FDR role models. Which is why I held out hope of one day being normal. Because I continually stoked the fantasy that one day I could be Jackson.

Part of me knew that wanting to be like Jackson was utterly preposterous. I can only attempt to explain it by proposing that its very impossibility lent it a sort of credence in that sort of counter-factual fugue state that is crucial to any hyper-intense relationship. Any relationship so intense that love and hate seem to combine to form a plasma cloud beyond the mere everyday states of matter of solid, liquid, and gas of mere friendship or even love. In short: Big Brother.

In Jackson's defense, he never signed up to be a father figure. Or even an uncle figure. Or even a big brother figure. And he certainly never signed up to be a big brother to a midget (or, if you prefer, "little person") who reacted to even the most gentle, looping pop fly by squatting down in fear and holding his baseball glove over his head like someone expecting an airborne tactical battlefield nuclear explosion or a hail of crossbow bolts. I cannot help but think that when Jackson was told he could expect a little brother he (not unreasonably) thought he could at least expect someone he could toss a football back and forth with, and not a person who, even if he had been normal sized, had such poor hand eye co-ordination he would be hard pressed to hit water if he fell out of a boat. On top of all that I was incapable of taking sports seriously in that terrifyingly earnest way that people who are serious about sports seem to have such a visceral need to. In the way that only makes it that much more ridiculous to everyone who doesn't experience that need. I don't know at what point Jackson finally threw in the towel on his hopes of having a younger brother he could teach sports to, and then trounce at sports for his own amusement. Which is really the only point of having a younger brother. I wasn't even good enough at sports to be trounce-able in any meaningful way. I was completely useless. So I strongly suspect that Jackson gave up on me around the time I started recognizing "the look": an expression of utter, shattering disappointment every time I took a swing at a slow pitch that wouldn't have busted a grape, or had a football lofted to me with all the intensity of a beach ball bounce painfully off my extended finger tips for the millionth time. And it was only later that I began to blame myself. To believe that if only I had at least made an attempt to be something, if even on a tackling dummy level, that maybe Jackson would've stayed with me on Pontactico, and not run away to study, and live among, and get eaten by the Kwakiutl.

$ $ $

I did not grow up outwardly normal, like Jackson. This was a simple reality of genetics: Jackson was tall and strong and good looking. I was zero for three in that department. I grew up weird. Or, perhaps more charitably, I grew up outside the statistical mean. Outside the juicy, ooey-gooey center of the bell curve. Nature or nurture? At this point in my life I'm not sure I can compel myself to care. I accept and forgive myself for growing up with an absentee Father, a sex addict and a manic depressive, the contents of a menagerie, and Itsy-Bitsy Bourbon Pissing FDR and Gay Sasquatch as role models. Not that there is anything wrong with Gay Sasquatch. Or Itsy-Bitsy Bourbon Pissing FDR. But I cannot have a meaningful conversation with an Itsy-Bitsy Bourbon Pissing FDR. Because all that Itsy-Bitsy Bourbon Pissing FDR can say is snippets of quotes from the real, full sized, non-bourbon-pissing FDR. His most memorable speeches. As if

I am pulling a string out of his back: "We have nothing to fear, but fear itself!" over and over and over again. Inspiring, the first hundred or so times you hear it. But lacking in the sort of nuts and bolts way that might aid me in the day-to-day workings of my life. Gay Sasquatch would've been a terrific role model. If I had known he existed. But I did not know he existed. Until he saved my life from Gay Time Traveling Hitler that last Thanksgiving in Tiny Town, on Pontactico.

$ $ $

I'm not saying my uncles were bad people. It's just that I saw them once a fucking year. And if they thought there was anything strange about my Kasper Hauser lifestyle, they kept it to themselves. Besides, as I came to understand later, being a manic depressive or a sex addict can be a full time job. Add to that being a manic depressive whose only support system is a sex addict (and conversely, being a sex addict doing what he can do to look after a manic depressive in his down time from sex addicting) and there are simply not enough hours in the day. Still, it was Uncle Roo (the manic depressive) and Uncle Dash (the sex addict) who (sadly) probably had the closest relationship in our immediate family. Granted it was a relationship based on charting Uncle Roo's manic episodes and tracking Uncle Roo all over the world as Uncle Roo used his enormous portion of The Van Kruup Family Trust to fuel whatever manic delusion he was in the throes of at that moment. These biochemical walkabouts of Uncle Roo's tended mainly towards the fugitive-in-fear-for-his-life, Yasser Arafat never sleeping in the same house twice, Nazi high command fleeing the still smoking ruins of Berlin sort of model. During these runs, Uncle Roo could've beat Jimmy Hoffa in a game of hide-and-go-seek.

Uncle Dash's only clue to the state of mind of his brother Roo were the seasons: Uncle Roo's mental health seemed to have its own internal circadian rhythm. The human psychological equivalent of a cicada on a seven year breeding cycle. Spring would bring returning migrating birds, and the first stirrings of full blown mania in Uncle Roo. Autumn would bring majestic fall colors in the 10,000 acres of trees on Pontactico, Thanksgiving, and Uncle Roo doing a detonation implosion of a post-mania catatonic depression.

The short answer to why Father made his brothers, my Uncle Dash and Uncle Roo, show up every Thanksgiving on Pontactico, as far as I could determine before that final Thanksgiving, is "because he could". It was a little brother power move. Father was the baby of the family. But he controlled The Van Kruup Family Trust, on which Uncle Dash and Uncle Roo were entirely dependent. It was a double power move because Father could helicopter in to Pontactico. Uncle Dash and Uncle Roo had to drive in. And the only way to drive in was to navigate the abandoned rail spur that linked Pontactico to the outside world. Built back in the days when Uwe would travel around his far flung empire by luxury private rail car. Uncle Dash would have to drive Uncle Roo down the barely passable rail right-of-way in an all-terrain vehicle like someone ferrying a rich tourist to the mountain top ruins of an abandoned Inca city. Because by Thanksgiving, Uncle Roo was usually so shot, so deep in the Marianas Trench of post mania depression, paranoia, and permanent panic attack that getting him to fly in a helicopter was out of the question.

Not that Uncle Dash and Uncle Roo had a lot of pressing engagements to tear themselves away from. Strike that: they didn't have *any* pressing engagements. Aside from full-time sex-addicting and full-time manic-depressive-ing. They just didn't have any commitments to anyone other than themselves. Thanksgiving on Pontactico was basically the only time every year they had to be in any designated place at any designated time. As opposed to when Uncle Roo was in the full manic phase of his illness. And then (in his mind at least) he was supposed to be all places at all times, like a quantum particle. And then he would crash. Hard. And only had to be in one place at one time: Pontactico on Thanksgiving.

I did not see Trees coming. I did not see the end of Pontactico coming. I believed Pontactico was a snow globe, protected and frozen forever in time. Like the exhibits in the menagerie. Like the photographs of the Kwakiutl, Apache, Sioux, and Cheyenne in Edward Curtis's handsome, leather-bound, 20 volume set "The North American Indian". I had no reason to believe otherwise. No storm clouds on the horizon. No omens. No eclipse of the sun. But, like history, omens only seem obvious in retrospect. Which makes me re-think my reaction to Jackson fucking the 150-year-old sofa cushion in the library. If not an omen, it was certainly a warning. At least as portentous as a solar eclipse. But one can only make sense of these things in retrospect. Only after I put some sort of "Colonel Mustard in the Conservatory with a lead pipe" sort of narrative behind it. Only after it has been carefully infused with the magic power of a cause and effect narrative. The cause being, not Jackson fucking the 150-year-old sofa cushion in the library, but his reaction to seeing *my* reaction of uncomprehending astonishment he misread as judgment at him fucking the 150-year-old sofa cushion. The effect being a mortified Jackson leaving Pontactico to find something besides a 150-year-old sofa cushion to fuck. And ending up living among, and studying, and getting eaten by the Kwakiutl (volume 10, "The North American Indian: Sorcerers, Medicine Men, Warriors & Warfare, Kwakiutl Songs").

Thanksgiving was the closest the Van Kruup family ever came to being "the Van Kruup family". Which was close only in a horse shoes and hand grenades sort of way. Because Father refused to be a father and my uncles refused to be uncles and my big brother made it very clear he had no interest in being a big brother. Which left Gay Sasquatch. Who I didn't even know existed until that last Thanksgiving when he rescued me from killer Gay Time Traveling Hitler in Tiny Town. Which was, to my way of thinking, one of the great missed opportunities in my life. I found an Itsy-Bitsy Bourbon Pissing FDR on Pontactico. I found the dead, naked, pickled Pawhtnatawahta woman on Pontactico. I did not find Gay Sasquatch on Pontactico. Because Gay Sasquatch did not wish to be found.

Me and Gay Sasquatch only became friends after we both left Pontactico, and I admired him for his strength and wisdom enough to make him my Vice President when I became President of the Remaining States of America. And then when I became King of New York I appointed Gay Sasquatch interim President of the Remaining States of America. Gay Sasquatch was a trail blazer. He was the first openly gay President. He was the first openly sasquatch President. Gay Sasquatch met, and fell deeply in love with, and, in a solemn and tasteful ceremony, married Professor University, the masturbating Orangutan from the masturbating primate Houston Astros. They took up residence in the White House, with me, and we spent most of our time together, attempting to sort through the important and pressing issues of the day. Like how to stop the Chinese from mining our precious space garbage. And whether or not to hand over New York State to the Japanese.

Gay Sasquatch proved himself wise even beyond his years (he was 178 years old - vibrant middle age by sasquatch standards). And when I said he was strong, I mean that literally: often, at the playful insistence of the crowds of tourists outside the White House gates, he would single handedly overturn one of the armor-plated SUVs of the Secret Service. After which, of course, he would right-side it, and even the Secret Service officers would clap, as we had long ago run out of gasoline, so those armor-plated SUVs weren't going anywhere. He was also the only one who could restrain Professor University from masturbating with a compelling level of confused intensity during any official state visit from any official state visitor. Old habits die hard, and that's all Professor University could think to do when a crowd of more than a couple of people assembled before him. Which was usually the minimum when Gay Sasquatch turned an armor-plated SUV over, so for the tourists it was kind of a two-for-one deal

I wish I had known Gay Sasquatch was living on Pontactico. But Gay Sasquatch felt compelled to keep a low profile. Understandably compelled by what happened to so many other high profile former inhabitants of America (bison, passenger pigeons, the Pawhtnatawahta). And no one would've known he existed at all if someone hadn't taken that picture of Gay Sasquatch watching me jack off to the dead, naked, pickled Pawhtnatawahta woman dressed as Henry VIII, and then that picture hadn't appeared on the front page of every newspaper in America.

$ $ $

Naturally I wondered about the circumstances of my birth, and my family. But my curiosity had limits, like the wall that completely circled Pontactico, dividing it from the outside world. Why was Jackson tall and strong and good looking, while I was a midget (or, if you prefer, "little person"). Why did my father and uncles only visit once a year, on Thanksgiving? Why was I never allowed to leave Pontactico? Children come equipped with a single super power that ensures their survival under any, save the most abominable of circumstances: the power to normalize any situation. And that super power exists as long as there is nothing to show them that their situation is *not* normal. Or, at the very least, that it's not the only situation in the world. Pontactico, to me, was the only situation in the world.

Which was no problem as long as I had Jackson with me. But then Jackson decided he needed another situation. A situation that needed the world outside Pontactico. Because the world outside Pontactico was the only place Jackson could find people to have sex with and play sports with. And the Kwakiutl. So Jackson began his voyages of exploration and discovery. His first expedition of cultural anthropology. To the town of Frenchmans Bend. Which, of course, made *me* want to go to Frenchmans Bend to see what all the fuss was about. Which I assumed was a relatively low reading on the fuss-o-meter. An assumption which, it turned out, was correct. Because I did not want to have sex or play sports. Which, it turned out, were the only things to do in Frenchmans Bend.

Jackson, from the outset, attempted to discourage me from leaving Pontactico. Jackson portrayed the world outside Pontactico as a world of danger. Potentially lethal danger. Lethal danger that he, as Big Brother could only be trusted to understand and he, as Big Brother was the only one who could be trusted to deal with. Stepping foot off Pontactico, for me, seemed to involve instant and irreversible misfortune and most likely violent death. And he had case studies to back it up: the heir to the Getty Oil fortune, John Paul Getty II being kidnapped for ransom, chained in a hole, and having his ear cut off and sent in the mail to his grandfather, the founder of Getty Oil. And the Kennedys all getting shot down like dogs by both individual maniacs and entire cabals of sinister forces. He did not tell me about the story of Michael Rockefeller, who left his home to live among, and study, and get eaten by, the Asmat people of Papua New Guinea.

$ $ $

I was born (I assume) on Pontactico. I say "assume" because, like Uwe, I can find no real record of my existence. I can find none of the detritus of my childhood. No baby pictures. No bronzed baby shoes. I do not remember my mother. For that matter I do not remember my father other than his spotty, indifferent visits to Pontactico. For that matter, come to think of it, I barely remember Jackson. Even my memories of Jackson come in fits and starts, like flashes of lightning. I assume I was born on Pontactico. I assume Jackson was born on Pontactico. Then again, I assumed Uwe, our family patriarch lived here on Pontactico, in the one-third scale mansion he constructed, but I can find no clues to support my assumption.

I assumed Uwe created the menagerie, but why? Again and again I am faced with the scenario that I am simply building a careful, causal narrative about me, Jackson, Uncle Roo, Uncle Dash, and even Gay Sasquatch. But Trees taught us one important lesson: history is bunk and the future was not terrorist attack, worldwide pandemic or asteroid strike, it was Trees. And even if we could see all the causes, all the effects, I'm not convinced it would matter. Even when the truth is in front of us, unvarnished, we cannot believe that the universe could be that callous, random, and indifferent to our well being.

Jackson once told me a story about the Tlingit, a neighbor of the Kwakiutl. When the first European sailing ship arrived on their shores the Tlingit did not have a clue what to make of it. They had no point of reference. So they assumed the great billowing sails were Raven, the trickster, come back, as he had promised he would. It was the only thing they could peg it to. Which is how I felt watching Jackson fuck that 150-year-old sofa cushion: I knew something was coming down the pipe, and I didn't exactly have a good feeling about it. But I also knew I was powerless over the changes that were coming. They were seismic. I knew it, and from the look on Jackson's face, he knew it too. But to beat a dead horse, *how* did he know that what he was doing was not exactly All American Sex Drive material? I mean, I read the expression of embarrassment on his face, but what did he have to be embarrassed about?

$ $ $

I was aware people had parents: a mother and a father I believe was the working model. But only as a sort of biological necessity. I just had no idea what those mothers and fathers were supposed to do in terms of a day-to-day reality. I had never witnessed a mother or father in action, doing mother and father type things (whatever that might consist of). I knew in a hazy way what they were supposed to do. Like if someone asked you what a rocket scientist or a marine biologist did. You could probably give the broad strokes. But you would have no picture of what their day-to-day routine consisted of. The sort of real world actions, responsibilities and results that were expected of them.

"Uncle" seemed fairly straight forward: fuck other men's wives, shoot your load on a cracker, go nuts, buy a permanently airborne atomic-powered 707 and show up once a year on Pontactico, on Thanksgiving. But the role of father was always a head scratcher to me, and seemed to consist of trying to make the best of a bad situation you really had no intention of finding yourself in, with no clear plan of attack on how to deal with it. Like someone who one day receives a letter in the mail informing them they have just inherited a traveling circus. The overall vibe of fatherhood seemed to oscillate with a force field of a doomed undertaking, half-grasped and ill-informed, like someone setting off on an expedition to the South Pole in tennis shoes and Bermuda shorts, with roughly equivalent results.

If Trees taught America (and, in the interest of inclusion and in the tradition of my "Big Tent" Presidential philosophy, the Remaining States of America) one thing, it's the nature of the universe to be completely normal and consistent right up until the exact moment it becomes the exact opposite of normal and consistent (partial checklist: Trees, Gay Sasquatch, Itsy-Bitsy Bourbon Pissing FDR, Jackson fucking a 150-year-old sofa cushion, the Chinese mining our space garbage). And then becoming so the exact opposite of normal that you cannot remember your previous, state of normal as anything other than a fog of memory. Up until that last Thanksgiving, Pontactico (op. cit. Itsy-Bitsy Bourbon Pissing FDR, Jackson fucking the 150-year-old sofa cushion etc.) was normal to me. Pontactico, everything on it, and everything that happened there, was my only frame of reference. Jackson's expeditions to Frenchmans Bend allowed him to gradually acclimate to the world outside Pontactico's version of normal. Like a man establishing base camps at higher and higher elevations prior to an attempt on the summit of Everest.

I have mixed feelings about Jackson going to Frenchmans Bend alone. Part of me feels like he had his hands full attempting to assimilate to a world where any wrong move might be his last, but he had no way of knowing what a wrong move was until he had potentially fucked up beyond repair. And before he made any move, he had to determine if something like fucking a 150-year-old sofa cushion was a wrong move (a subject which I cannot believe it would be easy to slip casually into a conversation). So in my defense, without even the benefit of the most basic debriefing about what I could expect outside Pontactico, how was I to know that a midget (or if you prefer, "little person") dressed as Napoleon showing up in Frenchmans Bend might attract any untoward attention? What really bothered me was that, without any initial frame of reference, before he even visited Frenchmans Bend, Jackson felt instinctively I was too far out for Frenchmans Bend. Which leads me to the obvious conclusion that I must have been weird even by the standards of Pontactico, a place he had proved the weirdness of himself, beyond doubt, by fucking a 150-year-old sofa cushion. Clearly he was in no position to point fingers. According to Jackson's implied judgment, I was weird not only by Frenchmans Bend standards, but by Pontactico standards, which were lofty indeed.

Who are you? Where did you come from? Where are you going? Sorry if that feels a bit accusatory. Today I am feeling touchy, exposed, and embarrassed. All luxury emotions. Embarrassment, in particular seems like an anachronism. A hold over from the BT world. Like having the option of cholera-free drinking water. And not being raped, tortured, and left for dead in the course of your day. Being raped, tortured, and left for dead seems to me might breach the levy of what embarrassment might be said to safely contain. We now live in a world where feigning death after being raped, tortured, and left for dead is considered a valuable life skill. Like knowing how to change the oil in your car was considered an important life skill BT. Certainly more relevant, AT, than long division. A world where "catamite" is an in-demand trade. A world in which weird is the new normal. But there has to be a point in your career as a catamite where "catamite" simply becomes your new normal. Where being raped, tortured, and left for dead becomes the new normal. Anything can become normalized given enough time and repetition. So time is irrelevant. Weird is our only metric. The only metric worth paying attention to, AT.

But even weird, like space and time, is a relative concept. Literally: my family was weird. But only by BT standards. Before being raped, tortured, and left for dead standards. But I only found this out after leaving Pontactico. From outward appearances my family seemed normal: Uncle Dash and Uncle Roo were so similar as to be almost identical. They were both tall and good looking. But there the similarity ended. Uncle Dash always showed up in expensive, perfectly tailored suits. Even when he showed up wearing a jet pack. Uncle Dash always looked fit and strong even in his fifties. Uncle Roo, by contrast, showed up dressed like an autistic Zouave, his weight see-sawing wildly from scarecrow to department store Santa in training.

Uncle Dash was present in the superficiality of his actions: eating, drinking, playing sports, and fucking. Uncle Roo seemed to not be present even when he *was* present. Like a man traversing the world in a deep sea diving suit: present in body only. Or a man gingerly picking his way across a minefield or attempting to defuse an atomic bomb while you were at the same time trying to maintain small talk.

By that last Thanksgiving, when Father was President of the Remaining States of America, most remaining Americans were asking "who are we?" and "where are we going?".Which don't seem like questions happy people ask. Happy people are too busy being and going. America was having one of her overly dramatic existential crises. The sort of over dramatic crisis of self-examination we never seem to understand that everyone who is not us finds head-achingly boring. America looks to her presidents to define and embody their age. And eerily, for the most part, that seems to happen. So when I became President on that last Thanksgiving after Gay Time Traveling Hitler killed Father, I found myself caught in an endless feedback loop of crippling self-conscious self-examination. I wanted to offer the American people a vision of their future: something equal to putting a man on the moon, a New Deal, a Great Society. But I knew about as much about the American people as I did about the Kwakiutl. Probably less. Instead I found myself dressed like Kaiser Wilhelm II complete with pickelhaube, jerking off for the Kennedys. Comes the moment, comes the man.

$ $ $

I never got the chance to tell the American people about Gay Time Traveling Hitler jerking off in Tiny Town. Which I think was probably a stroke of luck considering how they responded to seeing Itsy-Bitsy Bourbon Pissing FDR. I don't know what they could've done that would be worse than freaking the fuck out and crashing the Funk Market. Civil War? Revolution? I never got a chance to share my vision of America with America. I had high hopes. Those high hopes lasted two and a half weeks: until I addressed Congress and Itsy-Bitsy Bourbon Pissing FDR pissed an exact one ounce shot of bourbon on live national television and crashed the Funk Market. When I became President I insisted on knowing all the Presidential level underpants soiling presidential secrets. Where Gay Hitler came from was not one of those underpants soiling presidential secrets. So while I could tell the American people about Gay Sasquatch, and Jackson fucking a 150-year-old sofa cushion, and Itsy-Bitsy Bourbon Pissing FDR, I could not tell them about Gay Hitler. And I never got the chance to tell them that Killer Gay Hitler was itsy-bitsy.

$$\$ \ \$ \ \$$

Of course today everybody knows about Itsy-Bitsy Peppermint Schnapps Pissing Gay Hitler. Everybody knows what a pain in the ass Itsy-Bitsy Peppermint Schnapps Pissing Gay Hitler is. Literally: because almost everyone in this AT, Remaining States of America world knows someone, or knows *of* someone, or has seen first hand (God help us) someone (usually an Itsy-Bitsy Bourbon Pissing FDR, Itsy-Bitsy Vodka Pissing Stalin, or Itsy-Bitsy Gin Pissing Winston Churchill) raped, tortured, and left for dead by an Itsy-Bitsy Peppermint Schnapps Pissing Gay Hitler. But I did not know this was their MO when I was first confronted with an itsy-bitsy mob of enraged Itsy-Bitsy Peppermint Schnapps Pissing Gay Hitlers that last Thanksgiving. But I could tell from the itsy-bitsy evil glint in their itsy-bitsy coal black eyes they intended me ill-will (and by "ill-will" I mean "raping me, torturing me, and leaving me for dead").

$$\$ \ \$ \ \$$

If me and Father had both died that last Thanksgiving, if we had both been raped, tortured and left for dead by the Itsy-Bitsy Peppermint Schnapps Pissing Gay Hitlers, I'm not sure who would've become President. Like the DEFCON levels and the military command structure, I kind of zoned out when they were telling me about the government structure, and who was above who, and who would be President if the President and Vice President were both killed. Again: I figured the odds of this happening were about as close to zero as was mathematically possible. I assumed the Joints Chiefs of Staff would sort it out. Because they seemed to be comfortable with the DEFCON levels and knew the military command structure inside out. I just remember them staring at me with a look of utter, uncomprehending disappointment when I could not remember the most basic bullet points of being a Vice President. The same look Jackson used to give me when he realized I would be about as useful as a football bat to him at sports. I began to recognize that look of utter, uncomprehending disappointment all too well as I became Vice President, and then President. It always hurt, but eventually I began to get used to it. I began to expect it. Because I began to understand there was no way I was ever going to learn the DEFCON levels or the military command structure or who became President if both the President and the Vice President were killed, or learn to feign even a passing interest in sports. I began to expect the look of utter, uncomprehending disappointment everywhere I went and with everyone I met. I thought the American people would be glad to meet their new President. The American people were not glad to meet their new President. Especially when their new President began unloading brutal, unflinching truths on their asses. And wearing an EAT THE CRACKER T-shirt while doing it.

$ $ $

I wanted to know what my family was doing every Thanksgiving in Tiny Town that I was not allowed to be a part of. But I think mostly I wanted to know whatever they were doing, it had nothing to do with the extensive collections of 3d stereoscopic pornography in Tiny Town. I did not know what I would do if I found out that what they were doing involved the 3d stereoscopic collections of porn. Probably the same thing I did when I discovered Jackson fucking the 150-year-old sofa cushion: nothing. But I wanted to know. Because how was I to know that family circle-jerks over stereoscopic 3d porn wasn't a part of every traditional American Thanksgiving? How was I to know that the culmination to every Kennedy Thanksgiving in Hyannis Port didn't involve a circle-jerk along with a bracing swim in the North Atlantic, sailing, and touch football? Because it *did* seem to involve them watching a midget (or, if you prefer, "little person) jerking off for them while dressed as Kaiser Wilhelm II complete with pickelhaube.

$ $ $

Even if I had been able to tell the American people about the Itsy-Bitsy Raping Torturing Leaving For Dead Hitlers, I would not have been able to tell them *why* Itsy-Bitsy Raping Torturing Leaving For Dead Hitler wanted to rape me, murder me, and leave me for dead. The obvious answer: because I had tried to kill him? Stay with me: every time travel scenario involves traveling back in time to kill Baby Hitler. But odds are if you have access to time travel, almost by definition everybody else must have access to time travel. Which means Hitler must have access to time travel. Which means Hitler must have no choice but to travel forward in time to kill everyone who's trying to travel back in time to kill him as a baby. I can't really back any of this up. It's kind of just a hunch.

$ $ $

I went to Tiny Town that final Thanksgiving mainly because I was sore at never being invited to go to Tiny Town on Thanksgiving. It never occurred to me that there was a good reason for not being invited to Tiny Town. That maybe it was for my own good. That maybe my family was trying to protect me. And I can state unequivocally that I did not think it was to protect me from killer time traveling itsy-bitsy Hitlers. But they *were* trying to save me from killer time traveling itsy-bitsy Hitlers. Or save the world from killer time traveling itsy-bitsy Hitlers. Or something. I never really found out. I could not tell you if a major is above or below a captain. I could not tell you if DEFCON 1 meant "all clear" or "get ready to see your entire family reduced to a cone of cigarette ash in the nanosecond before your liquified eyeballs run down your cheeks". And I cannot tell you for sure why my family was in Tiny Town that final Thanksgiving trying to kill all the killer time traveling itsy-bitsy Hitlers.

$ $ $

Facts, direct personal experience: I cannot share my direct personal experience about that final Thanksgiving in Tiny Town. Because I'm still not entirely sure what happened that final Thanksgiving in Tiny Town. Fact: Tiny Town was full of Itsy-Bitsy Peppermint Schnapps Pissing Killer Hitlers. Fact: Father, Jackson, and Uncle Dash in his jet pack were all attempting to kill all the Itsy-Bitsy Peppermint Schnapps Pissing Killer Hitlers. With baseball bats. Why were they trying to kill all the Itsy-Bitsy Peppermint Schnapps Pissing Killer Hitlers? I do not know. Because Father, Jackson, and Uncle Dash are all dead. Brutal, unflinching truth: I do not wish to go in to the brutal, unflinching truth about what happened that final Thanksgiving in Tiny Town. Because I did not get a chance to see the final outcome of what was happening that final Thanksgiving in Tiny Town. Because as Father, Jackson, and Uncle Dash were busily dispatching Itsy-Bitsy Peppermint Schnapps Pissing Killer Hitlers with baseball bats, I found myself cornered by Itsy-Bitsy Peppermint Schnapps Pissing Killer Hitlers. Itsy-Bitsy Peppermint Schnapps Pissing Killer Hitlers wielding rusty nails, straight razors, shards of broken glass, scraps of rusty tin cans, and sharp-ened sticks. And my family didn't even know I was there until I had been cornered in the alley behind the tiny bowling alley in Tiny Town, and screamed for my life. And I realized that all the howling Itsy-Bitsy Peppermint Schnapps Pissing Killer Hitlers would get to me before my family could. Which is the exact moment when, out of nowhere, Gay Sasquatch, wearing a TOO FAT TO GO TO THE MOON T-shirt ran in like a linebacker scooping up a fumble, cradled me in his enormous hairy arms, and sped off with me to safety.

Chapter 6

I awoke this morning in The Egg, in Albany, with a truly Presidential bourbon and grape soda hangover following a truly Presidential bourbon and grape soda drinking binge (or, if I am still the King of New York, a *royal* bourbon and grape soda drinking binge?). I did not intend to have a presidential (royal?) drinking binge. But the bourbon and grape soda seemed to me to be the only defense against all the brutal, unflinching truth, all the facts and direct personal experiences contained in this memoir. I just wanted desperately to be done. To jam this memoir, dripping with all the brutal, unflinching truth in the shelves of the library of the Cultural Education Center between Martin Van Buren and George Washington (I think that's where it's supposed to go - my knowledge of the Dewey Decimal System is by no means exhaustive, even without a wincing bourbon and grape soda hangover).

$ $ $

In attempting to tell the events of that final Thanksgiving I became overwhelmed with the utter pointlessness of my task. Even if I did know all the Presidential Level Secrets (or even the Gay Sasquatch Level Secrets) I'm not sure it would make any more sense. And even if it did make sense, even if I do finish this and jam it in the library of the Cultural Education Center between Martin Van Buren and George Washington, who would ever find it? And even if they did find it, who would want to read the memoir of the only President who spent most of his life living in total isolation in the middle of 10,000 acres of forest and whose entire social circle consisted of his big brother and a pair of Irish wolf hounds. And an Itsy-Bitsy Bourbon Pissing FDR. Which no one finding this memoir today would care about, because Itsy-Bitsy Bourbon Pissing FDRs are everywhere. So I started drinking, thinking of all the time I've wasted on brutal, unflinching truth, and wondering where the fuck I was going to go and what the fuck I was going to do when I was done with all the brutal, unflinching truth. I started drinking and did not stop until Itsy-Bitsy Bourbon Pissing FDR stopped pissing: until he ran out of deliciously-oaked bourbon piss. Until I was left extending my empty highball glass in a gesture of pitiful, imploring expectation as Itsy-Bitsy Bourbon Pissing FDR sweated and strained and grimaced so hard that nothing happened except an itsy-bitsy vein in his itsy-bitsy forehead looked ready to burst and he emitted an itsy-bitsy, bordering on the ultrasonic, dog whistle of a fart. Then the Japanese blew up my memoirs.

$ $ $

The events of the last twenty-four hours seem more jumbled than the last twenty-four years. And for more reasons than can be accounted for simply by the bourbon and grape soda. Complicating factor number one: does blowing up my memoirs with the 16-inch guns of the USS Iowa count as an international incident? What DEFCON level should I inform my non-existent Chiefs of Staff to assume? What sort of Presidential response is required or expected? I do not want to be accused of Presidential over-reach. Somewhere back in the not too long ago I was sworn to defend the constitution of the United States of America. I think. And I vaguely remember something about "all threats, foreign and domestic". Which I believe must include the subset "the Japanese navy blowing up the memoir of the President of the Remaining States of America". But technically I am not living in the Remaining States of America. I am living in territory annexed by Japan following the Basketball War. New York is the new Puerto Rico. Also, the Japanese weren't trying to blow up my memoirs. They were trying to blow up my stuffed animal collection.

At some point last night I became convinced (or rather, the bourbon and grape soda convinced me) that, as part of my imaginary performance art piece "President Writing Memoirs" (as presented by The Egg, on the Empire State Plaza, in Albany - GET YOUR TICKETS BEFORE WE'RE ALL SOLD OUT!) I needed an audience. A performance piece audience: an audience of mannequins. Or rather, an audience of *one* mannequin. Because that was all I managed to drag into The Egg. Because you would not believe how hard it is to drag a mannequin. It would have been difficult if, like the mannequin, I was regular sized. But the mannequin outclassed me by at least a half dozen weight classes. Plus the fact that the swiveling arms and legs were constantly spinning around and whacking me in the knees, arms, and upper body, leaving me this morning covered in bruises, looking like someone tied me to a tree and pelted me with tennis balls or under-ripe apples all night. Which is why, naturally, I switched to stuffed animals.

The stuffed animals were from the carnival midway, on the Empire State Plaza. The carnival midway had been brought to the Empire State Plaza as part of the celebrations for my coronation as King of New York. I do not know what factory full of sociopaths on early work-release prisoners turned out these stuffed animals. The stuffed animals are disturbing. Throw the softball, knock over the wooden milk bottles, and win a disturbing stuffed animal for your girlfriend. "Disturbing" because it is difficult to even tell what animal they are supposed to be. Disturbing because their color palette runs from a strange purple resembling recently eviscerated internal organs to good old fashioned piss-yellow and shit-brown. All of which gradually began to dawn on me as I begin to sober up and "wouldn't it be funny if someone visited me and found me writing my Presidential memoirs in front of an audience of stuffed animals" turned over in my mind to the far more likely "nobody is ever going to visit me here, and if they do, it will probably be to rape, torture, and leave me for dead. And that the last thing that I will see as I am left to casually bleed out through every savagely violated orifice on my body on the stage of The Egg, in Albany, is an audience of disturbing stuffed animals and the blank, middle-distance stare of a single mannequin."

Almost as soon as I had this thought I became overwhelmingly embarrassed and self-conscious in the way that only spending too much time by yourself can produce. I became overwhelmingly embarrassed and self-conscious about the mannequin and the stuffed animals with me in The Egg. This was not entirely paranoia. Someone *had* taken that picture of Jackson having sex while I watched dressed as Napoleon in Frenchmans Bend. That, and the fact that the bourbon and grape soda had thrown in wild, self-pitying mood swings at no additional charge made me extremely angry and indignant. Angry and indignant enough to start dragging the stuffed animals out of The Egg and on to the Empire State Plaza, piling them on top of a bunch of car ties and then setting the entire jumble on fire like a Viking funeral pyre. Angry and indignant and self-pitying enough to forget how much the Japanese navy and their 16-inch guns hate bonfires. Angry and indignant enough to pull out my dick and start jacking it for anyone on the orbiting Empire State Building in orbit, if they so chose, to take a picture (I think when I was President this was referred to by my staff as "getting out ahead of the issue").

Whether or not anyone on the Empire State Building took a picture I cannot say. But the Japanese navy definitely took the opportunity to lob a 16-inch shell my way. And in that strange, counter-logical moment between seeing the barrel-flash of the 16-inch gun and the sphincter-tightening "FABOOOOOOOM" as the sound waves finally reached me, I realized if someone was taking a picture of me from the orbiting Empire State Building, they were about to take a picture of me getting blown into unidentifiable bits of skull, tooth, and bone shards on the Empire State Plaza (while jerking off). Which is the exact moment at which Gay Sasquatch tore out of the darkness of the forest surrounding the Empire State Plaza, scooped me up like a linebacker recovering a fumbled football, and carried me out of the blast radius of the incoming shell to safety.

$ $ $

Drunk, jerking off, in the wee hours of the morning, in the eerie reflected glow of a pile of burning, freakish stuffed animals, while perhaps not an ideal moment to re-connect with an old friend you haven't seen in some time, seemed, for me at least, charged with a certain reassuring symmetry, if not outright synchronicity. Besides, if your friend cannot accept finding you, following an extended absence, drunk, jerking off beside a pile of melting, oily black smoke emitting, disturbing stuffed animals, I might respectfully submit that perhaps they might not be a true friend. Or (extending the hypothesis) drunk, jerking off beside a pile of burning stuffed animals dressed as Henry VIII. Dressed as Henry VIII if he'd just survived some sort of extended stay on a desert island or penal colony. Being unable to find any clothing my size in Albany I just kept wearing Uwe's Henry VIII costume (which seemed like a no-brainer for my inauguration as King of New York) until it had begun to turn to rags on my body. All the other costumes I had left on Pontactico following our last-chopper-out-of-Saigon exit. I flatly refused the only other two options available to me: wearing children's clothes or wearing adult clothes cut arbitrarily down to size to fit my little person frame. Both of which I felt would make me look either infantilized or simple-minded. So every day, like the commandant of some long-abandoned fort who refused to give up his position, I put on my increasingly deteriorating, increasingly smelly Henry VIII costume. In the end I looked more like the King of the Hobos rather than the King of England.

I was partially astounded at seeing Gay Sasquatch and his Orangutan lover Professor University (and here, to put all rumor to rest, let me say that their relationship was no sordid inter-species tryst - that Professor University self-identified sexually as a gay sasquatch, as is his right, and therefore it was all perfectly above board) but I partially expected it as well. Because considering his history, I don't think I'm being overly dramatic when I say he's the one person you probably *could* expect to jump out at you, any time, any place. He had, after all, spent 178 years on Pontactico undetected by me. What Gay Sasquatch thought of my living conditions he kept to himself. But even stinking drunk I think I detected a nose wrinkle from Professor University as we embraced awkwardly, his enormous hairy arms encircling me in a tender (disturbingly concerned?) embrace. I realized to my horror that perhaps my standards of personal hygiene, following my extended isolation, may not have been up to even orangutan standards which, to be brutally and unflinchingly honest, are not exactly eye-wateringly high.

$ $ $

I said there would be no Presidential Level Secrets in this memoir. Here is a Presidential Level Secret (which, technically speaking, is actually a Gay Sasquatch Level Secret). Because it's everything Gay Sasquatch told me about Pontactico, and my family, both Pontactico and Post Pontactico. And AT. Because Gay Sasquatch has seen it all. Literally: Gay Sasquatch is 178 years old. Which is modest middle-age by sasquatch standards. And almost all of those 178 years were spent on Pontactico. So he literally saw everything: the who, what, and why of Pontactico. The "who" starting with Uwe, my Great-Great-Great-Grandfather, and ending with our escape from Pontactico following our run in with Homicidal Gay Time Traveling Hitler. Ending with Jackson running away to live among, and study, and get eaten by the Kwakiutl. Which brings us to our first Gay Sasquatch Level Secret:

"Your brother isn't dead. He's alive, and well, and living in Indianapolis."

At first I thought Gay Sasquatch was making a joke: insinuating something about the quality of life in Indianapolis. That it might be difficult to discern the subtle nuance between being dead and living in Indianapolis. Which brings up the obvious question, "why Indianapolis?" To which Gay Sasquatch replies: "because who would fake their own death and move to Indianapolis?". Which, I must admit, does have an almost water tight circular logic to it

But Gay Sasquatch did not travel to the Empire State Plaza in Albany to tell me Jackson is alive and well and living in Indianapolis. At least that's not the primary reason. The real reason is to tell me something almost as mind warping:

"The Pawhtnatawahta are not dead. The Pawhtnatawahta are alive, and well, and living on Pontactico." He tells me in the same flat, even tone as he told me Jackson is alive and well and living in Indianapolis. But he is not done. He did not arrive to simply drop this knowledge and amscray. He is on a mission. A mission to bring me back to Pontactico. Because Gay Sasquatch Level Secret No. 2: the Pawhtnatawahta are alive and well and living on Pontactico and the Pawhtnatawahta are traveling to outer space. And they want me to be President of the World.

$ $ $

These facts are coming at me hard and fast, to put it mildly. This is the first time I've ever played "Guess What Gay Sasquatch Knows!", and the Lightning Round answer of "that the Pawhtnatawahta are alive and well and living on Pontactico and going to outer space and want you to be President of the World!" is going to take some adjustment. But there is no time to adjust.

Because Gay Sasquatch has been dispatched by the Pawhtna-tawahta to escort me back to Pontactico. I am going to meet the Pawhtnatawahta on Pontactico. That is not an elocution exercise. In all my years on Pontactico, the only Pawhtnatawahta I knew existed was the dead, naked, pickled one in the menagerie. Now I am going to meet the rest of the Pawhtnatawahta. I pray to God the rest of the Pawhtnatawahta don't know about me jerking off to the dead, naked, pickled Pawhtnatawahta woman in the menagerie.

$ $ $

It occurs to me that these are all secrets that should go in my memoir. That I really *do* have Presidential Level Secrets. Even better than that: I have Gay Sasquatch Level Secrets. It occurs to me that my memoirs have been hit with a direct shot from a 16-inch shell from the USS Indianapolis. It takes me most of the morning to find most of the pages of my memoir, or what is left of them, scattered, singed and blown all over the Empire State Plaza. It occurs to me that there are going to be some holes (literally) in my memoir. It occurs to me that in a memoir that contains jerking off, Gay Sasquatch, Trees, The Great Funk Crash, me jerking off to a dead, naked, pickled Pawhtnatawahta woman, Jackson fucking a 150-year-old sofa cushion, the Chinese mining our space garbage, Gay Time Traveling Hitler, Itsy-Bitsy Bourbon Pissing FDR, jerking off for the Kennedys, and the Pawhtnatawahta traveling to outer space and making me President of the World, who the fuck is going to notice?

$ $ $

This morning, on the Empire State Plaza, in Albany, there's a lot of new information coming in. A lot to assemble into my new tinker toy called "the new normal". I can feel the normalization crew in my brain working overtime. You would think, after all that's happened to me, I would be an expert at converting the bizarre, the unexpected, into the norm. Not so. I am in the in-between phase, the most dangerous, terrifying part of normalization: the part where you have to come to grips with the fact that all the fucked up things you once thought were fucked up are now normal. But now new fucked up things are making the old fucked up things obsolete. And you are therefore free to see the old fucked up things now as fucked up. Because the new fucked up things are now clamoring to be normalized. Because there are only so many things that can be normalized at one time. So the old normal becomes the new fucked up. This is just the reality of the universe. I don't make the rules. The new normal: my big brother Jackson is alive and well and living in The Lost City of Indianapolis, the Pawhtnatawahta are alive and well and living on Pontactico, the Pawhtnatawahta want me to be President of the World, because the Pawhtnatawahta are traveling to outer space. Commence normalization sequence...NOW!

$ $ $

The arrival of Gay Sasquatch in Albany has brought my memoir-ing to an end. Because I am no longer talking about things that happened (past tense), but things that are happening now (present tense). Which means this is no longer a shitty, half-assed memoir. It is a shitty, half-assed diary. Dear diary: today Gay Sasquatch showed up in Albany to tell me the Pawhtnatawahta want me to be President of the World. I do not know if Gay Sasquatch is communicating an actual job offer or making a simple aspirational statement, part flattery, filled with touchingly childlike over-enthusiasm. I am given no job description, no list of rights and responsibilities. Will there be a formal transition of power from the former World President? Gay Sasquatch informs me the Pawhtnatawahta wish to avoid a power vacuum.

A power vacuum, apparently, that is the result of *not* having a World President? I was not aware that a lack of World Presidents constituted a power vacuum. No wonder we've been floundering all these years.

$ $ $

I am to travel to Pontactico to meet the Pawhtnatawahta. And become President of the World. There is a power vacuum. But from whom is the power transitioning? Granted I haven't exactly been moving in the elite power circles in Albany, but it's a head scratcher. It seems to me that the only time we need a President of the World is in bad science fiction movies when the interstellar alien invasion dreadnoughts show up and turn the day to night with their numbers and announce through their darkly comic public address system "TAKE US TO YOUR LEADER!" to everyone and no one in particular simultaneously. Have I been nominated to grovel for our puny lives before our new alien overlords? To beg not to have our children abducted and shipped off to alien slave colonies? If I am President of Earth, does that mean there are other presidents of other planets? Am I to traverse the vast emptiness of deep space to other galaxies to glad-hand other mock-human, Swiftian abominations and satirical pseudo-worlds which will allow me to realize the absurdity of the human condition: racism, sexism, will-to-power, ecological collapse? Various bad science fiction cliches flash across my mind: awkward greetings with sentient gasses, doomed interspecies love triangles, and endless shimmering panoramas of potential utopias doomed by all the usual suspects (racism, sexism, will-to-power, ecological collapse).

I do the long division of the ever-repeating remainder that is the contemplation of an infinite universe: the universe (being infinite) must mathematically contain an infinite number of scenarios. By definition, being infinite, it must contain *all* possible scenarios. And therefore (and here, like a mad scientist attempting to fit the final lines of their impossible proof on a chalkboard before running out of space entirely) must contain every possible premise that could only charitably be described as "bad science fiction cliches". You know, things like Itsy-Bitsy Bourbon Pissing FDRs, macaroni and cheese bushes, a Gay Sasquatch, the Chinese mining our space garbage, and putting the Empire State Building and Statue of Liberty into outer space.

$ $ $

Gay Sasquatch informs me we are to leave Albany immediately and to travel to Pontactico. We set out after a hearty breakfast of macaroni and cheese and boiled passenger pigeon eggs. I pack my memoir. I pack my Blivits. I pack my manual typewriter. I plan to keep track of our journey Marco-Polo-style. I think this is a sound comparison. Everybody thought Marco Polo was full of shit too. Maybe Lewis and Clarke is a better model. We are the Lewis and Clarke expedition of our day. If the Lewis and Clarke expedition included a Gay Sasquatch, a midget (or, if you prefer, "little person"), an orangutan named "Professor University", two Irish wolf hounds, and an Itsy-Bitsy Bourbon Pissing FDR. It's a scene I hope to see someday portrayed in heroic soft focus painted on the inside of a state legislature's capital dome. I think it would certainly be more entertaining than the usual wagon trains heading into heroic sunsets.

$ $ $

I'll spare you the details of my trip to Pontactico. Here are the details of my trip to Pontactico: Trees. The entire trip basically consists of me staring at the impenetrable bush three feet in front of my face, riding Gay Sasquatch like a back pack, trying not to get motion sick as Gay Sasquatch leaps and ducks and sprints his way through the forest. His movements are a sight to behold. At least they would be if I wasn't too busy trying not to get clotheslined by low hanging branches that would take my head clean off, leave me a smear of teeth and eyeballs on the branch of some unyielding, low-hanging oak or maple branch. When we stop at the end of the day I feel as if I've just spent the last eight hours inside a cement mixer.

We progress west, Professor University swinging through the forest canopy far above us, Romulus and Remus flanking us. We are headed for Buffalo (the city, not the large, frightening hairy mammals who have returned in abundance like the passenger pigeon). We are headed for Buffalo under a blazing canopy of blazing orange and red autumn leaves. In July. Because: Ice Age (because "Trees"). One detail: the sky above New York is filling with passenger pigeons. They are headed east, toward Albany. Which makes me glad I'm headed west, away from Albany. Because Albany, and The Egg in Albany, and all of the Empire State Plaza in Albany are about to be covered knee deep in passenger pigeon Shit.

I am eager to get the full story of Pontactico and of my family, from Gay Sasquatch. But Gay Sasquatch is busy keeping a weather eye out for whatever AT, hastily assembled rape-murder-leaving-random-Americans-for-dead society we might inadvertently stumble upon while crashing through the bush on our way to Pontactico. And the question of why every human society seems to spontaneously, either in whole or in part, reassemble itself into some version of raping, torturing, and leaving for dead its fellow apocalypse survivors keeps running around my head. I'm pretty sure Gay Sasquatch could take care of himself if we were to stumble upon our fellow post-America Americans bent on inflicting some combination of the above mentioned post-America options. My main fear is that, if the proverbial shit were to hit the proverbial rape, torture, left-for-dead fan, I might be the first thing jettisoned to increase his personal odds of escape, like a hot air balloon pilot dropping their ballast of sandbags while attempting to crest a particularly challenging mountain peak.

$ $ $

Turns out Buffalo is not on the express route from Albany to Western Pennsylvania and Pontactico. Pittsburgh, however, is. In a roundabout way. I think. After a few days whipsawing through the bush on the back of Gay Sasquatch, I feel I would be lucky to remember my own name, let alone draw a detailed map of the eastern seaboard. In addition to not having a dictionary I also do not have an atlas. Whoever pillaged the library in the Cultural Education Center on The Empire State Plaza must've been a stickler for facts, geography and correct spelling. Was it the same person who left me my manual typewriter with no capitals and a worn out exclamation point? What's the connection? I guess it fits with the whole "someone obsessed with QUESTION ASKED! QUESTION ANSWERED!" scenario. No room for error with all those capitals and exclamation points. Once a question is ANSWERED! walking it back is not really an option. Honestly, right now I have other things on my mind. Like not being raped, tortured and left for dead by a Buffalo Bills-themed rape-torture-leaving-random-Americans-for-dead gang. Somehow that image just springs to mind: that whoever is left in the crumbling cities of America would need something to identify with. Some badge of tribal loyalty. It seems a natural fit. A way to distinguish yourselves from all the other rape-torture-leaving-random-Americans-for-dead gangs that would be crawling about the wreckage of America looking for canned goods and fellow Americans to rape, torture, and leave for dead. But again: my geography is terrible. It would not be a Buffalo Bills-themed-rape-torture-leaving-random-Americans-for-dead gang. It would be a Pittsburgh Steelers-themed-rape-torture-leaving-random-Americans-for-dead gang. Still, take it all around, it has to be better than getting raped, tortured, and left for dead by a Cleveland Browns themed rape, torture, leaving-random-Americans-for-dead-gang.

$ $ 4

At night we make camp, giddy with relief at successfully eluding whatever NFL themed, rape, torture, leaving-random-Americans-for-dead gang we might have crossed paths with. We need the campfire. The Ice Age is coming. The passenger pigeons are coming. Bit by bit the story of my family, Pontactico, and the Pawhtnatawahta seeps out of Gay Sasquatch and I attempt to get it all down on my wonky, manual, punctuation-impaired typewriter, with its fading typewriter ribbon and strategic reserve of typewriter paper. Important historical fact number one: the Pawhtnatawahta are not exterminated like the passenger pigeon and the buffalo. They are alive, and well, and living on Pontactico. Which means, to my enormous embarrassment, they were alive and well and living on Pontactico while me and Jackson were alive and well and living on Pontactico. It flashes through my mind they are alive and well and know about me and the dead, naked, pickled Pawhtnatawahta woman in the menagerie, on Pontactico. And that maybe they are not impressed with me and the dead, naked, pickled Pawhtnatawahta woman in the menagerie, on Pontactico. And maybe that's the real reason why I'm being summoned to Pontactico. It's one of those subjects that is hard to bring up in casual conversation. I decide never to bring it up in casual conversation.

$ $ $

This was supposed to be a story about America and jerking off. A memoir: by an important member of an important American family. Kennedy important. Rockefeller important. But America is no more and my family is no more (freak jet pack accident, stepping down the elevator of the Empire State Building, not eaten by the Kwakiutl but alive and well and living in Indianapolis). It was supposed to be a memoir by a former President of the Remaining States of America. Now it is a memoir by a future President of the World. I'm not sure if that's a step up or a step down or a horizontal move. I'm not sure what that means in terms of finishing this memoir, or which section I should stuff it in the library of the Cultural Education Center ("Biographies, Presidents, America"?) between Van Buren, Martin and Washington, George. I'm not sure if I need to start another section in the library of the Cultural Education Center ("Biographies, Presidents, World"?). Which depresses me. I was hoping to finish this memoir and vanish it into the regular old Presidents of the United States section of the library of the Cultural Education Center. I am happy being a footnote in the history of the more noteworthy Presidents ("Who was the fattest President, the shortest President, the youngest President, which President was in office during the Basketball War?" - answers: Taft, me, me, and me). I'm not sure I am ready or even equipped to take on my new powers. Assuming my new powers exceed anything above the "World's Greatest Grandpa" level. I start to wonder exactly how anyone would react to me stumbling out of the bush, begging for food and water, while informing my rescuers I am the President of the World. Would they even take me seriously? I guess they would probably take me about as seriously as I took the Duke of Indianapolis when he showed up for my coronation in Albany. Snap executive decision: I am going to keep the whole "President of the World" thing to myself.

Everything I need to know about the world I learned from the menagerie. But everything I need to know about my family, the Van Kruups, I am learning from Gay Sasquatch. On our way to Pontactico. To accept my nomination as President of the World. At least I *think* I'm going to accept my nomination as President of the World. I do not know what responsibilities the job will demand of me. Hopefully not having to remember what those fucking DEFCON levels mean, or I'm going to be buying a ticket on the first express Gay Sasquatch back to Albany. Am I allowed not to accept my nomination? That might be awkward. Believe it or not, despite everything that's happened to me, I'm not a fan of awkward. Which means I'm going to accept my nomination for President of the World simply not to be rude. Not to be embarrassed. This from a man who has had a picture of him jerking off to a dead, naked, Pickled Pawhtnatawahta woman dressed as Henry VIII while Gay Sasquatch watched published on the front page of every newspaper in America. This from the man who spent most of his adult life jerking off to a dead, naked, Pickled Pawhtnatawahta woman while the real Pawhtnatawahta were alive and well and living on Pontactico and is now on his way to meet the Pawhtnatawahta on Pontactico. If I ever find the dictionary that guy with the punctuation issues stole from the library of the Cultural Education Center, I'm going to paste my picture next to the definition of "awkward".

I said this memoir would have no Presidential Level Secrets. But that was before Gay Sasquatch showed up and saved my life on the Empire State Plaza in Albany. And brought all his Gay Sasquatch Level Secrets. At night, beside the campfire, Gay Sasquatch begins revealing to me all his Gay Sasquatch Level Secrets (BURN AFTER READING?). At night, beside the campfire, I type out what Gay Sasquatch tells me. Right now, I am typing out what Gay Sasquatch tells me. Here is what Gay Sasquatch is telling me:

Chapter 7

The Van Kruup story is only partly a story about America and jerking off: Uwe coming to America after the Civil War to jerk off for paying customers. Sort of. The bullet points: Uwe Van Kruup did not amass a fortune; Uwe Van Kruup did not use that fortune to build Pontactico. The Pawhtnatawahta used Uwe Van Kruup to build a fortune. And they used that fortune to build Pontactico. Which means this is not a memoir by an important member of an important American family. We are not the Kennedys. We are not the Rockefellers. We are not even the Carters or the Clintons. Which means I am not even Billy Carter or Roger Clinton. This is not even a memoir by a half-wit member of a so-so important family (apologies Billy Carter, apologies Roger Clinton, that was overly harsh).

Uwe's story was an American success story. If it was actually Uwe's story. Historical footnote: it is not Uwe's story. It is the Pawhtnatawahta's story. It is a rags to riches story. Kind of. At the very least it is a "dressed as Napoleon, Kaiser Wilhelm II, Julius Caesar, Henry VIII to Pontactico" story. Which I admit does not have the same luck and pluck ring to it. It might be shoe-horned into the "ragtag band of misfits" narrative of American history ("Give me your tired, your hungry, your wanting to jerk off dressed as Napoleon, Kaiser Wilhelm II, Julius Caesar, Henry VIII" - I think that's the gist of the inscription on the side of the Statue of Liberty). Uwe arrived in America speaking no English. With a trunk full of costumes. With a new immigrant's wild-eyed mania to take his shot at the American Dream. And with a hitch-hiking micro-organism called "spirochete treponema palladium": Uwe arrived in America with a case of neurodegenerative syphilis.

$ $ $

I have seen photographs of people with neurodegenerative syphilis: in the medical texts in the library on Pontactico. Word of advice: do not look up "neurodegenerative syphilis" in the medical texts in the library on Pontactico (or any other library for that matter). I do not remember all the symptoms of neurodegenerative syphilis listed in the medical texts in the library on Pontactico. And I do not intend to refresh my memory by looking them up in the medical texts in the library on Pontactico. The main symptom of neurodegenerative syphilis (if memory serves): neurodegeneration. On the macro level: fecal and urinary incontinence and dementia. Neurodegenerative syphilis makes you go crazy and shit yourself, not necessarily in that order. But the medical texts, as far as I can remember, did not list "jacking off in period dressed as Napoleon, Kaiser Wilhelm II, Julius Caesar, Henry VIII" as one of the symptoms of neurodegenerative syphilis. So this is not a story about America, and jerking off, and one of America's most important families and one of America's most important fortunes. It is a story about going crazy and shitting yourself. I think I have discovered an entirely new sub-genre of the Great American Success Narrative. As long as America now considers going crazy and shitting yourself a success.

Gay Sasquatch does not know exactly how Uwe came to America. Or exactly why Uwe came to America. Uwe's history, pre-America, is a black box. Presumably America was not conducting an active program to recruit Europeans who were going crazy and shitting themselves. That might be a little bit outside the mandate of the inscription on the side of the Statue of Liberty. But Gay Sasquatch knows how Uwe came to Pontactico. But before that I have to tell you about the Pawhtnatawahta. And before that I have to tell you about Alsoomse. Because that is the name of the dead, naked, pickled Pawhtnatawahta woman. Also, I have to fit Wovoka and the Ghost Dance in here too. Although technically I don't think it really matters exactly when I fit the Ghost Dance in. Because: Ghost Dance. Hang in there. All will be explained in time. I think.

Gay Sasquatch knows all of the Pawhtnatawahta history. He has personally experienced 178 years of Pawhtnatawahta history. So Gay Sasquatch begins his story 178 years ago, give or take. Gay Sasquatch's Readers Digest Condensed History of the Pawhtnatawahta (volume 3: "The Last 178 Years"): 178 years ago was not a good time to be Pawhtnatawahta. Or Teton Sioux, or Yanktonai, or Plains Assiniboin. The buffalo was gone. The passenger pigeon was gone. And if all went to plan (small pox, repeating rifles, land theft) soon the Teton Sioux, the Yanktonai, the Plains Assiniboin and the Pawhtnatawahta would be gone too. Interesting historical footnote: the Teton Sioux, the Yanktonai, the Plains Assiniboin and the Pawhtnatawahta did not want to be gone.

The Pawhtnatawahta had spent the previous two hundred years playing an exciting game of hide-and-go small pox, repeating rifles and land theft. It was not a game they were winning (because "small pox, repeating rifles, land theft"). The Pawhtnatawahta figured an aggressive policy of "Stay The Fuck Away From the White Man" would allow them to escape the worst ravages of the White Man. It did not allow them to escape the worst ravages of the White Man. Because the White Man would not stay the fuck away from the Pawhtnatawahta. Soon the Pawhtnatawahta were squished into their tiny corner of western Pennsylvania with nowhere else to go, no place left in which to stay the fuck away from the White Man. After two hundred years of attempting to understand the White Man, the Pawhtnatawahta woke up one day to a detailed understanding of the White Man. Here was their detailed understanding of the White Man: "more". No matter how much the White Man had, it was never enough. There was always more to be had. Somehow, some way, there always had to be more. The main tool of more: "science". Science and technology were what allowed the "more": railroads, repeating rifles, steel mills. So the Pawhtnatawahta made a decision: they would do an end run around the White Man to the White Man's science. And that's where Alsoomse came in.

$ $ $

Before she was "the dead, naked, pickled Pawhtnatawahta woman", she was "Alsoomse", and she was selected by the Pawhtnatawahta to learn the science of the White Man, to help them figure out how to avoid going the way of the buffalo and the passenger pigeon. But this was not going to be easy. Alsoomse was the brightest and the best of the Pawhtnatawahta. She would travel out in the wide world and figure out what the fuck the White Man was up to. She would observe their law, their science, their technology, and report back. It didn't seem like it could be all that hard: as far as the Pawhtnatawahta could tell, science was all the White Man really had going for him. Alsoomse made it as far as Frenchmans Bend. Where she learned about White Man secret weapon number one: germs. Alsoomse caught a cold and died. That, it seemed, was the end of the Pawhtnatawahta search for the White Man science.

A year passed before the Pawhtnatawahta figured out what had happened to Alsoomse. Here's how they figured out what happened to Alsoomse: a year later a Traveling Circus of Absurdities and Oddities swung through Frenchmans Bend. Part of the Traveling Circus of Absurdities: a woman pickled in an enormous tank of formaldehyde called "Hippolyte, Queen of the Amazons!". Only it wasn't "Hippolyte, Queen of the Amazons!". It was Alsoomse, who was now the dead, naked pickled Pawhtnatawahta woman. Valuable lesson learned from discovering Alsoomse in Frenchmans Bend in an enormous tank of formaldehyde: if you do not hide the fact that you are Pawhtnatawahta (or Teton Sioux, Yanktonai, or Plains Assiniboin) no white man is under any obligation to treat you as if you were anything other than Pawhtnatawahta (or Teton Sioux, Yanktonai, or Plains Assiniboin). In other words, like people who were too big, or too small, or had lobster claws for hands, they could treat you any way they damn well pleased. The Pawhtnatawahta made a collective mental note: from now on they would keep the fact they were Pawhtnatawahta to themselves.

But the Pawhtnatawahta persisted, and they got the hang of science. And technology. And business. And finance. But it was all theoretical: only white dudes were allowed to science, technology, business and finance. They could not even buy the land they were living on and had spent the last 300 years playing hide-and-go-smallpox-repeating-rifles-and-land-theft on with varying degrees of success. To survive they needed to buy land, to buy influence, to buy protection. In other words, they needed to buy a white man. Enter Uwe Van Kruup.

The answer to the Pawhtnatawahta's problems showed up on their doorstep. Literally: Uwe floated down the Youghiogheny River to Pontactico from Frenchmans Bend. Inside his crate. Because everyone outside his crate had attempted to tear him limb from limb out of outrage when he showed up in Frenchmans Bend to jerk off dressed as Napoleon, Kaiser Wilhelm II, Julius Caesar, Henry VIII. The good people of Frenchmans Bend so did not want to see Uwe jerk off dressed as Napoleon, Kaiser Wilhelm II, Julius Caesar, Henry VIII, that Uwe had to go DEFCON 4 (DEFCON 1? BLUE? YELLOW? PURPLE? PAISLEY?) and seal himself inside his crate. So the people of Frenchmans Bend threw Uwe and the crate in the Youghiogheny River upstream from Pontactico.

Uwe and his crate floated downstream to Pontactico. Where the Pawhtnatawahta fished him out. The Pawhtnatawahta made use of Uwe almost instantly: to use their savings to use Uwe to buy the land Pontactico is on. Uwe gave them access to capital and gave them the ability to buy the beginnings of what would become the largest fortune in America. No, not the Van Kruup family fortune: the Pawhtnatawahta fortune. We are not rich.

We never were rich. The $367.32 in Blivits is possibly the most money the Van Kruups ever had in one place at one time. Everything belongs to the Pawhtnatawahta: Pontactico, The Van Kruup Family Trust, and all the moving parts of the Van Kruup family fortune: coal, oil, steel, railroads. And (I assume) jerking off, and garbage. Which I'm not sure does or does not matter. All the money in the world isn't going to turn back the Trees or stop the Ice Age or bring back America. Even if I still had access to The Van Kruup Family Trust, what could I spend it on?

Uwe and the Pawhtnatawahta reached an understanding. The Pawhtnatawahta would build Uwe a place to live and where he could complete his neurosyphilitic degeneration in relative peace and comfort. He would be tended to by a small army of servants (literally: all the servants were little people). Uwe would sign every document placed before him by the Pawhtnatawahta detailing the purchase of coal, oil, steel, and railroads with an increasingly spidery signature as his degeneration started getting up a full head of steam. Not part of the deal: the small army of servants running their own side hustle by taking pictures of Uwe jerking off in period costume. So when the Pawhtnatawahta found out, they fired all the little people servants. Hence the Chernobyl vibe of Tiny Town. Now they had no one to look after Uwe. But Uwe wouldn't need looking after much longer. His degeneration was almost complete. Which threw a spanner in the works for the Pawhtnatawahta. Because they *still* couldn't sign their own documents and own their land and coal, oil, steel, railroads. So they came up with an answer. This time they wouldn't buy a white man. They would make one.

The Pawhtnatawahta had been studying science. They had been studying it in the library and the menagerie on Pontactico. They had studied the white man science and got the hang of it without a great deal of trouble. They got bored with the White Man Science, so they began to invent Pawhtnatawahta Science. Which was a lot like White Man science. Only without the White

Man. Which made it better. Because: no White Man.

The Pawhtnatawahta decided they would make their own White Man. They would Frankenstein a White Man. The White Man would be based on Uwe, since he was the only White Man they had access to. Their first iterations (the Pawhtnatawahta would be the first to admit) were barely functional. When Uwe's presence in person was required for some reason, the Pawhtnatawahta were faced with the challenge of keeping Uwe up and running. Because, to their horror, every iteration of Uwe quickly went crazy and shit itself. Sometimes this took weeks, sometimes days, sometimes hours, but it always seemed to happen. They could never be one hundred percent sure their Uwes wouldn't (literally) shit himself at every meeting and legal signing they needed them for, so they had to keep at least a half a dozen identical Uwes up and running at any given time. Borrowing parts from each other like a teenager trying to keep an unreliable used car on the road. Eventually, they got better at making White Men, at making Uwes. But there was another problem: the Pawhtnatawahta, like any good Creator, had become enamored of, addicted to, creation. Addicted to making more Uwes. Then different versions of Uwe. Bigger versions. Smaller versions. Then, like any God, any Creator, one day they found they had wandered into the "Let's just see what happens if we put some of this in some of that/duck billed platypus/naked mole rat part of town. And then (eventually) the macaroni and cheese/Itsy-Bitsy Bourbon Pissing FDR part of town. And Trees. Because the Pawhtnatawahta science had one important element White Man science did not: Ghost Dance.

$ $ $

The Pawhtnatawahta may have summoned me to Pontactico, but there are no Pawhtnatawahta on Pontactico to greet me when Gay Sasquatch, Professor University, and me arrive. Everything on Pontactico looks pretty much the same as when I left Pontactico about a year ago. Unlike the world outside Pontactico, Trees didn't much affect Pontactico, because Pontactico was already pretty much nothing but Trees. Pontactico's transition from BT to AT was virtually seamless.

I didn't give it much thought on the journey here (being, as I was somewhat preoccupied by my goal of not being raped, tortured, and left for dead by an NFL themed rape, torture, leaving random travelers for dead gang). But now that I am here, the thought that the entire time I lived here, I was sharing Pontactico unknowingly with the Pawhtnatawahta(and Gay Sasquatch)fills me with a sudden vertigo of embarrassment. Especially considering there's an above average chance that both Gay Sasquatch and the Pawhtnatawahta know about my life long pursuit of jerking off to a dead, naked, pickled Pawhtnatawahta woman. At which moment a live, naked Pawhtnatawahta woman appears to welcome me back to Pontactico.

$ $ $

Not *exactly* a naked Pawhtnatawahta woman. An almost naked Pawhtnatawahta woman. A "may as well be naked" Pawhtnatawahta woman. A Pawhtnatawahta woman in a skin-tight, silvery, shimmering space suit. Not the sort of clunky affair that would actually work in outer space to prevent your insides exploding in the freezing vacuum of outer space like a water balloon thrown against a concrete sidewalk. The sort of space suit visitors from outer space in bad science fiction movies full of bad science fiction cliches wear. The kind of space suit visitors from other galaxies wear when they land their spacecraft on the lawn of the White House to demand to meet with the President of the World. Complete with a confused looking geometric logo smack on the chest like the piss-poor logo of an expansion NHL hockey team designed by some well-intentioned but fundamentally aesthetically tone-deaf sports marketing department.

She is tall. She is beautiful. She is totally ripped. Understandably: traveling across the universe, meeting alien beings on alien worlds, all while wearing a skin tight unitard must be a great motivation to pass on dessert. Either that or she is from another bad science fiction movie scenario: from the future. The sort of future where everyone wears the exact same clothes in a sort of fashion based egalitarian movement aimed at avoiding the present day pitfalls of our fundamentally flawed human existence (racism, sexism, will-to-power, ecological collapse). But if she is from the future, that means the Pawhtnatawahta have mastered time travel. Suddenly I have to suppress the fear that they have summoned me here to Pontactico to travel back in time and kill Baby Hitler.

$$ \$ \$ \$ $$

So where have the Pawhtnatawahta been hiding all this time? Why, when I became President, was I not told that the Pawhtnatawahta lived on Pontactico? Even Gay Sasquatch was holding out on me on that one. Which, to be honest, hurts. And how much did my Father and uncles and Jackson know? They knew enough to go to Tiny Town every Thanksgiving and kill Itsy-Bitsy Hitler. But none of them are here to answer for their actions. It's just me and the Pawhtnatawahta. And they are taking me to where they have been hiding for the last 150 years: across the Youghiogheny River (just over the one-third scale Rialto Bridge, hang a left at Tiny Town, tell 'em Stanley Astor Jazzhands Superstar Galaxy Gramophone Van Kruup III sent ya!). But before I am allowed to see where the Pawhtnatawahta have been for the last four hundred and fifty years, they must explain to me what they have been up to for the last 150 years: Pawhtnatawahta Science. I will not be allowed into the place where the Pawhtnatawahta Science has been cooking up Itsy-Bitsy Bourbon Pissing

FDRs and the entire Itsy-Bitsy Booze Pissing Yalta Conference. Because it would break my brain. At least I think that's the main thrust of what they're trying to tell me. No White Man could stand to see the real inner workings of the White Man's world. Which is what Pawhtnatawahta Science, give or take, explains. That is the main message (give or take).

$ $ $

When I became President of the Remaining States I was shown many things only the President is ever shown. I was taken to Roswell Air Force Base on Marine One, the President's official helicopter and shown the UFOs (plural) that crashed there and the bodies of their extra-terrestrial pilots. I shook hands with Gay Sasquatch beneath the moonlight under the rotunda of the Jefferson Memorial in Washington, DC. I was helicoptered to Greenbrier, the secret underground government bunker which was to be used as shelter in the event of global thermonuclear war. Now that I am about to be sworn in as President of the World, I assume I am going to be shown many things only the President of the World is ever shown. I hope those things will be more interesting than what I was shown when I became President of the Remaining States of America. I hope all will finally be revealed. I hope that this memoir might finally make some sense. I have thrown aside the "Deus ex machina" in favor of "Pawhtnatawahta ex Pontactico". But now the Pawhtnatawahta *cannot* show me all the secrets I seek even if they wanted to. As we cross the one-third scale Rialto Bridge and make our way past Tiny Town, we are joined by more and more Pawhtnatawahta women in shiny jump suits. We progress deeper into the forest, like some Victorian era explorer stumbling upon the Lost City of Eldorado, the inhabitants piling into the streets to stare at me. And then it suddenly hits me: they are all wearing the exact same silvery space suit, and they all look exactly the same. *Ex-*

actly. And there are no dudes. Not one. But just as this begins to register we have arrived at the place where the Pawhtnatawahta have been holed up for the last 150 years.

$ $ $

I can't say what I expected to be shown. Any more than I can tell you what I expected to be shown when I became President of the Remaining States of America. Which is exactly what I was shown when I became President of the Remaining States of America: the crashed UFOs at Roswell, Gay Sasquatch, and the underground bunker where me and my descendants would sip grape soda for the next thousand years waiting for radiation levels on the planet's surface to drop below instant-liquefica-tion-of-your-internal-organs levels. Which is why the first thing they showed me, on arrival at their state-of-the-art research facility in the woods just past Tiny Town, was something I *really* didn't expect: the UFOs that crashed at Roswell. Only their pilots weren't big-headed, big eyed weirdos. Because, as they explained to me, this was the *real* UFO that crashed at Roswell. And the real crew of the real UFO that crashed at Roswell weren't the interstellar spook show that I had been shown, that everybody more or less knows exists. The real crew of the real crashed UFO was Itsy-Bitsy Lando Calrissian, Itsy-Bitsy Apollo Creed, and It-sy-Bitsy Steve Austin.

$ $ $

The UFOs were itsy-bitsy. The crews were itsy-bitsy. And composed of fictional characters from shitty television shows and movies. I think we can both agree this was somewhat unexpect-ed. But there was more to come. Or rather, there *would* have been more to come if I wasn't a white dude. Because they keep trying to hint, to insinuate, to politely infer, that I cannot, under any circumstances, be shown what goes on inside their state-of-the-art research center in the woods of Pontactico. They insist my White Man brain will melt and run out of my ears (in as many words) if I am exposed to the Pawhtnatawahta science.

While they are trying to explain all this to me I am having difficulty focussing. Partly because I cannot seem to grasp what they are hinting broadly at. Partly because of the fact that I am surrounded by a small crowd of virtually naked Pawhtnatawahta women. Dressed in skin tight space suits that seem to engage every teenage boy bad science fiction interstellar sex fantasy cliche (I'll spare you the blow-by-blow). I am finding myself having the same feelings looking at the live, virtually naked Pawhtnatawahta women as I do looking at the dead, naked, pickled Pawhtnatawahta woman. I am aroused. Visibly. Which I guess is a good news/bad news scenario. Good, I guess, in the sense that I have discovered I am capable of being aroused by live human females. Bad in the sense that all the live human females I am being aroused by can see that I am being visibly aroused. Which is when Itsy-Bitsy Wovoka appears to attempt to clear things up.

$ $ $

Tactfully, Itsy-Bitsy Wovoka steers me away from the crowd of virtually naked Pawhtnatawahta women and we stroll about the grounds of the Pawhtnatawahta state-of-the-art research facility. The Pawhtnatawahta state-of-the-art research-facility is called "The Wovoka Center for Interstellar Exploration and Sentient Evolution". This is explained to me by Itsy-Bitsy Wovoka. The "Interstellar Exploration" part seems pretty self-explanatory. The "Sentient Evolution" part would seem to beg further explanation. I do not ask Wovoka for further explanation. Instead, I imagine what the T-shirt for The Wovoka Center for Interstellar Exploration and Sentient Evolution might look like.

"ITSY-BITSY UNIVERSITY" pops into my head. Since I assume this is where they made all the Itsy-Bitsy FDRs, Itsy-Bitsy Hitlers, Itsy-Bitsy Stalins, and Itsy-Bitsy Winston Churchills. And Itsy-Bitsy Wovoka? I am just in the middle of attempting by means of deduction and elimination to determine what sort of alcohol Itsy-Bitsy Wovoka pisses when I realize Itsy-Bitsy Wovoka is attempting to explain Sentient Evolution to me. So I miss the explanation of what Sentient Evolution is. So I cannot tell you what Sentient Evolution is. Other than making Itsy-Bitsy FDRs, Itsy-Bitsy Hitlers, Itsy-Bitsy Stalins, and Itsy-Bitsy Winston Churchills. And macaroni and cheese bushes. And Trees. Yes, "Trees". A Presidential Level Secret has finally been made available to me! The Pawhtnatawahta made Trees. But how? Sentiently Evolving Trees? I am having trouble keeping up. Then Itsy-Bitsy Wovoka drops his show stopper on me: Ghost Dance.

The Pawhtnatawahta had White Man science but they had one thing the White Man did not: Ghost Dance. The Ghost Dance: Wovoka had a vision that the world of The North American Indian would return to North America the way North America was before the White Man showed up. Trees would drive the Europeans back into the sea. The buffalo would return. The wild horses would return. They had only to keep the old ways and dance the Ghost Dance. This was a vision of the future. The Ghost Dancers of the future had shown it to him. Not one possible future: a future that already existed. So the Pawhtnatawahta asked the future Pawhtnatawahta what the future of the Pawhtnatawahta looked like. The future Pawhtnatawahta sent them an Itsy-Bitsy Bourbon Pissing FDR. Their future selves, the Pawhtnatawahta concluded, were not without a sense of humor.

The Pawhtnatawahta realized their future was a DIY operation. That the Ghost Dance could only tell them so much. So they combined science and the Ghost Dance. They built the menagerie and the library on Pontactico as part of their new state-of-the-art research facility (at least as "state-of-the-art" as "state-of-the-art" was during the Grover Cleveland administration). In short: they began to create. Their creations began to create. Their created creations Frankensteined (sentiented?). Weird shit was going down in the middle of 10,000 acres of forest in western Pennsylvania. Itsy-Bitsy FDRs, Itsy-Bitsy Hitlers, Itsy-Bitsy Stalins, and Itsy-Bitsy Winston Churchills would eventually be going down in the middle of 10,000 acres of forest in western Pennsylvania. The Van Kruups were going down in the middle of 10,000 acres of forest in western Pennsylvania. The Frankensteined creations escaped (as Frankensteined creations are wont to do). My family is their creation. The Van Kruups are Frankensteins. The Van Kruups are Golems (or maybe more accurately, the Van Kruups are cane toads, we are kudzu, we are zebra mussels). I am reduced to a game of existential twenty questions: what am I (what is the Van Kruup family) without our fortune, without the Van Kruup family? And more importantly: what *is* the Van Kruup family?

The Pawhtnatawahta and Wovoka do not appear to want to answer my question straight up. They do not seem to be *able* to answer my questions straight up. I ask to see what is inside Itsy-Bitsy University, but they insist it will blow my itsy-bitsy mind (they are too diplomatic to say it, but I know they are talking about my Itsy-Bitsy White Man Mind). But I have to know. I have to sneak inside Itsy-Bitsy University.

$ $ $

But before that there are some official matters to attend to. To my great relief I find out my first hunch is incorrect: the Pawhtnatawahta are not traveling through time. I will not be asked to kill Baby Hitler. They are traveling across space. And by that I mean Space with a capital "S". They're not going to mine our space garbage or hit a home run in the Houston Astro Dome on the moon. They are capital "S", capital "T" Space Traveling across the capital "G" Galaxy. And they wish to thank me for the mixed blessing of my Great-Great-Great-Grandfather Uwe Van Kruup. Personally, I think spirochete treponema palladium deserves more credit than me (and possibly Uwe). They are handing over Pontactico to me. They no longer need Pontactico. They no longer need their fortune. Where they are going, they insist, no one needs money. Without money, according to their conclusion, there is no sexism, racism, will-to-power or exploiting the ecology to the point of failure. I feel the urge to debate them on this point, but a bigger part of me simply wants to know where this place with no sexism, racism, will-to-power or exploiting the ecology to the point of failure is. But before I ask, I already think I have the answer: some place with no White Dudes.

$ $ $

Getting into Itsy-Bitsy University is far easier than I thought. All I had to do was insist on being allowed into Itsy-Bitsy University. Technically, with the hand over of Pontactico, Itsy-Bitsy University is included on the bill of sale. The Pawhtnatawahta attempt to dissuade me, but I will not be dissuaded. I have to know what's going on inside Itsy-Bitsy University. I have to know who I am and who the Van Kruups are and how they made Trees and macaroni and cheese bushes and all the Itsy-Bitsy Booze Pissing World Leaders. Finally, they relent. There is nothing they can do. Especially since the Ghost Dance has taught them one thing: nothing can stand in the way of the Ghost Dance, of a future already written. My entering Itsy-Bitsy University, apparently, falls under that category. Because I am about to do it? Because I have already done it? Again, I am still sketchy on the exact details of "Ghost Dance". It doesn't matter. Now is the time to enter Itsy-Bitsy University, to discover the secrets of the Pawhtnatawahta, to discover the secrets of the Ghost Dance.

$ $ $

When I regain consciousness after discovering the secrets of the Pawhtnatawahta and the secrets of the Ghost Dance, I understand the meaning of the phrase "ignorance is bliss". My brains have not liquefied and run out my ears. Not quite. But they may as well have. Because I now know why the Pawhtnatawahta did not want me to go into Itsy-Bitsy University. Because now I know that the Van Kruup family is not the Van Kruup family. Because my older brother Jackson, my Uncle Roo and my Uncle Dash are not Van Kruups. They are Pawhtnatawahta. Which leaves me and Father.

The Pawhtnatawahta attempt to talk me down. They offer what seems to be some solid advice: family is what you make it. Literally. Not in a soft-focus, inspirational poster, kitten hanging from a clothesline sort of way. They have offered to make me a family. Literally: to order. Just like they made the Itsy-Bitsy FDRs, Itsy-Bitsy Hitlers, Itsy-Bitsy Stalins, and Itsy-Bitsy Winston Churchills. They can make me any size family I want, they don't have to be itsy-bitsy per se. They can make my family be any kind of family I want, like choosing color swatches for upholstery. My new family can have everything my old family did not. They can be everything my family never could be: patient, kind, understanding. And in amounts of patient, kind, and understanding beyond what is normally allotted to most humans. I take the deluxe package: a big brother who likes me for who I am and does not care I have the athletic ability of a cinder block, who enjoys hanging out with me. I take a pair of doting uncles as a side. In short, a perfect family. That lasts about a week.

Brutal, unflinching truth: being social, interacting with even the most patient and understanding person is fucking exhausting after spending most of your life alone on your own private, 10,000 acre estate. My new family is kind, patient, and understanding. In other words, boring as fuck. Jealousy, envy, will-to-power, these are the things which fill up the idle hours of our existence. You would not believe how much free time you suddenly have without people to envy and resent. So when I tell them I am leaving Pontactico and I do not wish them to come with me they are all fucking patience, all fucking understanding, all fucking kindness. It makes me feel like I'm going to vomit.

$ $ $

The Pawhtnatawahta are going to Outer Space but I do not wish to hang around and see it. I have had Pontactico to the teeth. Also, I don't think there's going to be much to see, in terms of the pyrotechnics of a rocket blast off. Not like when Father blasted the Empire State Building into space from midtown Manhattan. My guess is that their journey to deep space has to do with those itsy-bitsy UFOs piloted by those itsy-bitsy Lando Calrissians, Steve Austins, and Apollo Creeds. Seeing my hangdog expression following the creation of my designer family, Gay Sasquatch and Professor University have told me they are adopting me, and I cheer up. I have come to realize that family *is* important. Too important to be left to chance and the whim of genetics. I hereby dissolve all bonds to the Van Kruups and the Pawhtnatawahta. I abdicate as King of New York. I resign my presidencies as both President of the Remaining States of America and President of the World. Apologies to the Pawhtnatawahta, but I am retiring to private life ("private life" consisting of traveling across the Remaining States of America jerking off for paying crowds dressed as Napoleon, Kaiser Wilhelm II, Julius Caesar, Henry the VIII, and Abraham Lincoln?). I hope to make it to the Lost City of Indianapolis. Where I will, as my final Executive Order, make Jackson President of the World, and therefore President of the Remaining States of America. Which I think is a fair penalty for faking his own death and not telling me.

$ $ $

I now consider this memoir finished and my debt to the historical record paid. I will not place this in the library of the Cultural Education Center. I will place it in the library on Pontactico. I am not returning to Albany (sorry Japanese, sorry 16-inch guns of the USS Iowa). I will forge west. Or south. Or somewhere. On my raft. On the Youghiogheny River. With Uwe's crate of costumes. Into the land foretold by Wovoka. The land I saw in my vision when I passed out in Itsy-Bitsy University. When I saw the Ghost Dance.

In my vision of the Ghost Dance the Pawhtnatawahta were (are, will be, always have been?) returning to reclaim their ancestral lands. They rode their ponies and drove the buffalo before them. Hordes and hordes of buffalo. There is buffalo and passenger pigeons and there is abundant game of all kinds. And there are Trees. And there at the back of all this dust and thundering hooves is Wovoka. He gazes at the returned world all around him, his broad, bronzed, handsome face beneath his wide-brimmed, tall, conical hat. He is looking at the world around him. The world that he knew existed all along. The world Wovoka saw as clear as day. And he is laughing his fucking ass off at me.

Zero Books

CULTURE, SOCIETY & POLITICS

Contemporary culture has eliminated the concept and public figure of the intellectual. A cretinous anti-intellectualism presides, cheer-led by hacks in the pay of multinational corporations who reassure their bored readers that there is no need to rouse themselves from their stupor. Zer0 Books knows that another kind of discourse – intellectual without being academic, popular without being populist – is not only possible: it is already flourishing. Zer0 is convinced that in the unthinking, blandly consensual culture in which we live, critical and engaged theoretical reflection is more important than ever before.

If you have enjoyed this book, why not tell other readers by posting a review on your preferred book site.

Recent bestsellers from Zero Books are:

In the Dust of This Planet
Horror of Philosophy vol. 1
Eugene Thacker
In the first of a series of three books on the Horror of
Philosophy, *In the Dust of This Planet* offers the genre of horror
as a way of thinking about the unthinkable.
Paperback: 978-1-84694-676-9 ebook: 978-1-78099-010-1

Capitalist Realism
Is there no alternative?
Mark Fisher
An analysis of the ways in which capitalism has presented itself
as the only realistic political-economic system.
Paperback: 978-1-84694-317-1 ebook: 978-1-78099-734-6

Rebel Rebel
Chris O'Leary
David Bowie: every single song. Everything you want to know,
everything you didn't know.
Paperback: 978-1-78099-244-0 ebook: 978-1-78099-713-1

Cartographies of the Absolute
Alberto Toscano, Jeff Kinkle
An aesthetics of the economy for the twenty-first century.
Paperback: 978-1-78099-275-4 ebook: 978-1-78279-973-3

Malign Velocities
Accelerationism and Capitalism
Benjamin Noys
Long listed for the Bread and Roses Prize 2015, *Malign Velocities* argues against the need for speed, tracking acceleration as the symptom of the ongoing crises of capitalism.
Paperback: 978-1-78279-300-7 ebook: 978-1-78279-299-4

Meat Market
Female Flesh under Capitalism
Laurie Penny
A feminist dissection of women's bodies as the fleshy fulcrum of capitalist cannibalism, whereby women are both consumers and consumed.
Paperback: 978-1-84694-521-2 ebook: 978-1-84694-782-7

Poor but Sexy
Culture Clashes in Europe East and West
Agata Pyzik
How the East stayed East and the West stayed West.
Paperback: 978-1-78099-394-2 ebook: 978-1-78099-395-9

Romeo and Juliet in Palestine
Teaching Under Occupation
Tom Sperlinger
Life in the West Bank, the nature of pedagogy and the role of a university under occupation.
Paperback: 978-1-78279-637-4 ebook: 978-1-78279-636-7

Sweetening the Pill
or How we Got Hooked on Hormonal Birth Control
Holly Grigg-Spall
Has contraception liberated or oppressed women? *Sweetening the Pill* breaks the silence on the dark side of hormonal contraception.
Paperback: 978-1-78099-607-3 ebook: 978-1-78099-608-0

Why Are We The Good Guys?
Reclaiming your Mind from the Delusions of Propaganda
David Cromwell
A provocative challenge to the standard ideology that Western power is a benevolent force in the world.
Paperback: 978-1-78099-365-2 ebook: 978-1-78099-366-9

Readers of ebooks can buy or view any of these bestsellers by clicking on the live link in the title. Most titles are published in paperback and as an ebook. Paperbacks are available in traditional bookshops. Both print and ebook formats are available online.

Find more titles and sign up to our readers' newsletter at http://www.johnhuntpublishing.com/culture-and-politics

Follow us on Facebook at https://www.facebook.com/ZeroBooks

and Twitter at https://twitter.com/Zer0Books

Printed and bound by PG in the USA